Strawberry Angel and the Bean

PRESS

Strawberry Angel and the Bean

A love story, as old as time…

Roy Thomas

Books may be ordered through booksellers or by contacting:

1331 press – Black White & Read
PO Box 228
Wondai
Qld 4606 Australia

1331 press – Black White & Read. Details found on roydow.com
BWR - 01 (Black White & Read Series).

With Thanks.
Jason Williams, who assisted in the editing process, and provided valuable feedback on the content.
Kieran Benson, for much needed assistance in Layout & Typesetting.
Yvette Bentata-Moore.
Thank you all for being there.

Cover and layout design – in-house

ISBN: 978-1-922499-01-1 (print book)
ISBN: 978-1-922499-00-4 (e-book)

1331 press – Black White & Read.   rev. date: 2209-2020

Note to the Reader:
My intention with this book is to entertain, and sow seeds of light and love. If either is achieved, I am truly humbled.

To Polly and Amy, with love

Introduction

Welcome, to a world of wonder, welcome to a world of fun

Here i've conjured up for thee, a story set in winter sun

A story where there's much to see, if you would open up your eyes

And at the end it's there again, more reminder than surprise

To follow then a story of a seed (*the bean*), and what he does

On with fairies, mind the witches, wands that spew forth plasma fuzz

See, if *you* can find what Morris Mole discovers, there within

How to silence Glandwey Goblins dogs, that make an awful din

Strawberry Angel, darling fairy calls to you, that you may go

Upon a journey deep within, to find the light and love you know

Sowing seeds with words in rhyme of love and light to fuel the fire

Deep within the hearts of lovers, growing always, one desire

Merddyn waits, to take your hand, to help you then, discern your way

That you would always walk in light, so love will always fill your day

Perhaps there's nothing more to say, except to wish you on your way

And hope and pray, that you will see, the light that always shines in thee

~*~

1

Here then starts the story, of the angel and the bean
Of light and love, and life expressed, in essence so serene
Of how these things did come to pass and why we all must see
Inherent stuff within us all; to find, descend the tree

The clock of sexagesimals goes on and ticks away
A sixty here, a sixty there, all sixties fade away
Around and then around again, man's comfort in the tick
Expressions then, with order, only love will heal the sick

So on to quest for love and light, a story bound in life
'Tis said that good and evil balance either side of knife
The truth as seen on solsbury hill, the mirror twin of love sublime
A plan, a truth, a whim, a wish, guided by the light divine

A quest for golden glory, liken honey in the pot
The milk of human kindness, mix the same, the lovers knot
Entwined within the self-proclaimed, a lover free and true
Spied by merddyn, watched in love, and guided *dans la rue*

Stories hidden, words in words, the artful steer away
To keep the smile, that of *the keeper*, safe most every day
With twists 'n' turns, a nod, a wink, the answer plain to see
'Tis *here* the light of love makes a discoverer of *thee*

Thread the needle, find the eye that sits atop thy head
Seven days the journey, keep it pure for heavens bed
Pictures form within the mind, a dark and inner journey true
Composed from word in rhyme, I hear the monthly quest begins anew

The time is right, the moon has tracked a way into your sign
Love and light are what you see, the *all* your heart entwine
Life is swallowed, peace is found, a light atop your resting face
One slight transgression, love profound, tears fabric, forming space

~*~

2

Just off the coast of ancient lands, a druid sits in time and space
To take the faith-full by the hand, and help ensure they run the race
With balance then to truly see, if this is such a space in time
To find the ready so inclined, to seek what e'er their heart will find

Listen here, just listen, as we hear the murmur of the eight
The hand that takes a card or two, no deck is stacked enjoy your fate
Hear the voice of ancient wonder, care and love like of above
Here I see a seeker comes, a shadow falls with distant love

Each a thread to weave the patterns, weave the patterns of our life
Twists and turns, a choice encounter, leads to glory, leads to strife
All can come, and all can wonder, truth relieves the need for guile
Take a turn and seek the silence, in the darkness sit a while

There within to chant a question, chant a question of the flame
Answer then, the hearts reflection, up is down, it's all the same
Searching for it, where's the power, find the power in the love
Hear a whisper in the ether, guided then; does hand fit glove?

Chance to see the colours, vivid colours of delight
Perhaps to see a balance, not a wobble left or right
A time approaches of a cycle, start to sit amongst the twelve
Find a simple heart's desire, in the self, begin to delve

There's no echo, none from time/space? just from space/time here and now!
Strong vibrations from another, innocence is showing how
Time to walk a way to new awareness, transmutations
Feelings of the dawning of a time for celebrations

Heavy is the shadow of an energy so dark
Agony, despair and opportunities for love are stark
Anger and the fires of hatred, best be careful, steps beware
Swiftly on to mind the seekers, "mindful piggy, have a care"

"Yes, yes - yes, I see the way, the journey I will start today
Balance hearts and lay some thread, while resting easy in your bed
There are roles for them to play, a game enjoyed most any day
Well almost, 'cept when meanies lurk, about the place to act as jerk"

"But who am I to judge or label any who would play the game
And seek within, their growth enabled, by a hand that's of the same
All entangled in confusion, full of wonder, full of fear
Build desire within the darkness, seek the quiet voice come near"

"To speed across the land and sea, to co-create the journey done
By night my path is lit by moon, by day, i'm nurtured by the sun
To shift in shape and blend in form, see expectations as the norm
To hear and see as others may, guarded insights as we play"

"And so, *it* begins... "

~*~

3

W hat wonders thee when tired you are, and seek to lay thy head
Of what may be before us; should we ponder of the dead?
And how we always seem to miss the bridge to rest and play
And yes, we may reveal all truth before we see that day

In truth I come before you, with a truth, as truth it be
Of how each one of us was tricked, 'oh, perspicacity!'
Yet here we are now gathered, for a tale is here to tell
Pause, be present, take a breath, be sure to listen well

The veil of darkness turned to light, removal of the same
As history, all the stories gone, no need to play the game
Simple things, for things there are, to do and be and see
Gather up thy wits dear friend, compile a list for thee

'Tis true, the quest divine is real, a quest each bean can take
Fuelled by love and pure desire, to search is no mistake
Here we see it all unfold, and you will witness true
How this can be the way for beans, for all beans just like you

So enter now a world we know, for there is much to see
And listen out for all the truth, for that will set you free
Belief and love will always guide you, always show the way
All you have to do is listen, then your heart is on its way

Down and down from up on high, we cast our eye below
First we need to find a seeker, one to witness, one to show
There's another, knows the secret, keeps the ways and loves you true
Feeling safe, the love around you, guiding hands are here for you

Merddyn, faithful timeless walker, love and laughter all his days
Always watching for the seekers, here to guide with all his ways
Felt the timing for another, winter solstice come in days
Moon is rising, feeling full, a special day then, full of praise

~*~

4

In a house, at base of mound, a hill for sure was there to see
Its twin so close, to balance out the songs of love, the heart set free
Solsbury for a boy of wonder, seeker true with faith in mind
Silbury is the seat of balance, here the love for two inclined

In the kitchen stood the mothers, expectations spoke as true
Time and teaching not for nothing, each will grow, become brand new
Faith and reason, love to cherish, truth in paths for all to see
Here's the plan, divine in nature, as for them, so you and me

Sharing peace in meditations, finding freedoms that we share
Fast, the hunger cometh not, seek the righteous, have a care
Present, as your mind will wander, up and down a thought of yours
Dedication to the seeking, understand these simple chores

Soon enough the time's upon us, innocence in youth explore
Each will seek to find another, there beyond the darkest door
Truth is, there's no *special* needed, just intent and passion, yes
Time to understand the balance, there's no sin, so don't confess

Seek to know all served before you, all before you, there to dine
On the ravages of torment, as you seek to tame your mind
Carnal nature, great destroyer, great destroyer of the soul
Tethers you to all your senses, ever blurring of the goal

Unconditionally loving, mothers, fathers all, 'tis true
Taking time to help our children, as ourselves we surely do
Sharing moments of alertness, share the wonders of our sight
Steel the passion found in purpose, hold on all, with all your might

A silver light within a moment, one of twelve, around anew
Cycles here to help the sinner, see the innocence in you
Understand and see all error, as a learning meant to see
Hold the truth within your focus, see how it will set you free

On the precious thirteenth birthday, time to start the seeking ways
Stepping deeper into darkness, stepping deeper all your days
Simple is the process, there's no need for tools or pill
Know that you are on your way, just powered on by will

For *will* is all that you will need, and none can take away
That, which you begin to search for, on this very special day
Harken unto history? don't look back nor look ahead
Simply breath the love inside you, always there within your head

As evening came and darkness spread, all tired folk took to their bed
And while some sleep and some may dream, not all our nights are so serene
Toil and torment form the day, and then can form the night
Approaching all with love in mind, will surely end your plight

The bean, asleep, prepares for wonder, love and light will answer true
The age has come for revelations, seeps into awareness new
Meditations, pause, consider, step by step and all will see
Build your faith in sweet surrender, watch this bean descend the tree

How has such a young creation come to shine as though brand new?
Space and time for him were given, paths uncovered, trod by few
Teaching of the sky's reflection, inner pathways safe and near
Practice then within the silence, seek the quiet voice to hear

Careful then, the front desire, carnal mind will see you fed
Sweet and fatty, dark creations, heavy burdens, then you're dead
Special times need preparations, naked foods, a master hand
Find the balance, leap the hurdle, water soaks our desert land

Merddyn spots the young pretender, young pretender? are you sure?
His mind, it searched, and found a seeker, there beyond the old oak door
He steals into a darkened house and seeks the sleeper where he lay
To weigh the truth and error, knowing each is never far away

The weight of time and effort shows its mark upon this man
Our seeker and our guide, this man it be, I know he can
And as for merddyn, time is precious, never would he waste
His time on someone cutting corners, treading sacred paths in haste

And so, the seed divine begins to grow inside the heart
Stimulated by desire, will ne'er again depart
Not that it was ever gone, and all should know this true
This is the path of light and love, it beckons unto you

Unto all this path is open, never mind your faith and creed
Simply walk into the darkness, there your soul finds food to feed
Always searching in the quiet, in the quiet of your mind
Would you mention to another what you see and what you find?

Here was found a bean of substance, stout in heart, in faith so strong
Built up over years of practice, calm and silent in the throng
Knowing then the moment, moves with stealth, to seek the next
Innocence is confidence, no need to feel perplexed

Merddyn took a hook and landed, strand of man, of time and life
And laid a trail of all the moments, details of the pain and strife
Up the side of rainbow mountain, twists and turns laid out to see
Pure in heart this youthful seeker, strand near straight, he's nearly free

Seeking truth in all the error, turn when e'er we want we can
Pause our life and change direction, guided by a higher plan
Seek to bridge the gap to higher self by pure devotion
All the tools we have, divine they are in innovation

The young bean, here with purpose, paused in life through dedication
And chose this moment, through his birth, to spark his evolution
The moon for many, speaks with purpose every now and then
With fast 'n' focus, 60 hours; your spine will bring you zen

There's more to tell here, best rise up to glean a better view
Of scallywags and dirty deeds, a plot to mangle you know who
'Tis rumoured that an animal would seek to see it all
Just like a bean enlightened, from confusion disenthral

For though this pig, it cannot fly, it sees much more than names imply
With help from up on high, the very air supports the claim
The rook, the raven, crow perhaps, darkness seen in all the same
Aware, the watcher on the wing, first the eye, then voice will sing

Who's seen here and who's seen there and gossip floods in everywhere
We're travellers all with tales to tell, with magic see the interest swell
For always, as the time is right, there's things discovered out of sight
Of mind not eyes and so we see, from darkness there's a light in thee

Believing he can run the race, the count aspires with no disgrace
The first of all god's creatures seen, to deign to walk with steps serene
Reserved perhaps or so they say, for just the beans who walk this way
Or maybe energy is such, that *it* is all things, pretty much

If so, then just to be *aware* is all you need to be,
And understand the power of love and all that means to you and me
What form could an awareness take to satisfy poor you
Who doesn't know an arse from elbow, sad to say I feel it's true

This time then; well here's a chance, an opportunity to take
To read on slowly, mind the image, see the pictures words can make
Take an idea deep within, swallowed whole, absorb it all
All is new and just for you, so just jump in and have a ball

~*~

5

From out the darkness of a dream, a place of still and wonder true
Did first I catch a glimpse of thee, and thee of i, to see was new
That knowing deep inside, once felt, can never send away
A love that sparked so true and pure, then captured me that day

Strawberry angel, darling fairy, tell me that it's true
Speak it true thy love for me, as though you always knew
'Tis now mine eyes did find you, like you came from far away
And instantly lock onto to you, to dream you every day

For evermore, within my heart, a place for you is made
And always will it sing for thee, where e'er your head be laid
'Tis sad i'll never share these loving thoughts of mine with thee
For you are of a kind so rare and always must be free

Good morning strawberry angel, darling fairy that you are
Is this a curse upon my life to see you from afar?
To never feel the glow of love that stems from warm embrace
That feeling, with a look from you… and no, there is no trace

And so, I am content to simply see you everyday
To offer help and guidance as I do for all the rest
I hear the beating of my heart, I hear the things you say
The racing and the pounding like it's breaking from my chest

The truth is, i'm no different from a dozen, maybe more
And with so many loving you it could become a bore
But you, you are too pure to take for granted so much love
You recognise and hold on high the gifts from god above

For like us all, a lesson learned was on the cards for thee
To understand a little more of what there is to see
To grow in worth of self, 'tis true, and what you mean to me
And clearly hold the truth to side, for truth will set you free

~*~

6

So here's the tale of love and light, the fairy and the bean
Of how one came to hold the lamp of light that's never seen
And how a pulse of light and love brought freedom to the land
Then how our actions freed the souls that number as the sands

For now's the time, the great salvation, waters on his back
An age of wonder here upon us, say goodbye to lack
Focus on the individual, say 'i'm alright jack'
Then help still more to find the secrets hid inside the sack

You turn the page, but know this true, intentions here for thee
See the labour, see the work, embrace this gift from me
Sweet words in rhyme to chase thee on, to fly high like a *dove*
Then know your father's grace and favour, purpose, light, and love

Embrace the secret in your heart and find the purpose so brand new
Apropos of nothing maybe, fearless love will then ensue
Is this the only way? a question, not for me a penny bet
There's no other for you, maybe, seek awareness, cast your net

Every dawn is different, every yawn and every stretch is new
Seen through many different eyes, and so unique the point of view?
For when it's all, as all it is, the view's the same, but not for sense
For sense is such to anchor here, as though were stranded, tied to fence

Embrace the new, the weird, the strange, the challenging and see
That there is so much in this world, with time to see when free
Go embrace a word creation with a notion based on love
Get a feeling of elation, on the soaring wings of dove

Sit in moments daily, based on all you feel, to fill your sail
Think of parallels in space, seek a lesson, there's no fail
Who did this and that and what, and all the things that we saw done
And thoughts as fabric laid in time, all nurtured by our loving sun

So mindless then, so many, maybe all, at time in space gone by
As weakness framed on fear, which fed on nothing, for no *thing* was known
The catalyst, a timeless guide, and error then is always grown?
Not always, no, for choose we can, illumination of the eye

Observe a journey, sow the seeds of hope, forever in the hand
There's no conqueror, no castle keep, there is no sense, there is no land
If you could, would you, will you, have you? expectation's co-creation
Be in love with all the forces that you feel, the inspiration

~*~

7

Strawberry angel, darling fairy, came to me one day
"What's the problem strawberry darling, frost won't go away?"
She turned and gave an "ooh", you see, I gave her such a start
Which caused in me a chuckle, fidget, tickle, burp and fart

She blinked three times, and then twice more, then squinted tight at me
Twas strange to think this darling fairy couldn't see, dear me
Next, she washed a pane of glass that clearly wasn't there
She blinked again, then rubbed her eyes and scratched her gorgeous hair

"You can't see me, you can't hear me, it's as if I wasn't here
Yet clearly you see something, it's a mystery I fear
Stranger still you hear no sound, least not that I can tell
And so, cannot from me perhaps, but what about the bell?"

Elder flower slowly stood and walked towards a tree
Once there, he reached around the back where no one else could see
He found a spot and reached inside, he sought to hear the knell
To trick sweet strawberry angel with the sacred fairy bell

The bell was made of love and light, but radiated love
'Tis said that it was crafted by the hand of god above
Twas gifted to the fairies for safe keeping, now you know
A task of love for human beans, to help them when they grow

"I thought that that might tempt you, strawberry angel, and it did
But you must say to no one, you might know where this is hid"
He slowly bent with bell in hand and placed it on the grass
Translucent with a secret power, looked like it was made of glass

Strawberry angel smiled, giggled, walked towards the bell
"I can see you elder flower, rest assured 'tis true,
That i would never tell another, told me things by you
I like these games we play dear ef... "

"Dearest darling strawberry angel, i've no game to play today
But you could help me with another, someone special one could say
I've a task of grave importance, grave importance, yes that's true
Dangerous, some might consider, except of course if they were you"

"For someone such as you, sweet strawberry, you might see this as your fate
It is for you and only you, for you must keep this lover's date
And i cannot explain there further, not a smidgen, so you see
Questions here will never serve you, unlike having faith in me"

"Oh ef, dear ef, you play with me, just like you always do
You lay the truth upon the ground, then with distraction you bestrew
Just tell me ef, what is it that you wish that i should do
So that i may appear less like the story's ingénue?"

Strawberry angel gently flew up in the air and roundabout
Behind the back of elder flower, who took a step beyond the bell
The fairy paused, inspects the bell, no whisper, word nor shout
("I always knew her tongue would wag, for here's a tale to tell")

"It seems a shame to hide it so", sweet strawberry said to me
"To keep it hidden there within the hollow of that tree"
"All is done with purpose", said I, to the strawberry maiden fair
Mesmerised by flowing magic, there disguised, her gorgeous hair

Twas as she spun, i waved a hand, not once but thrice, to quell the light
Her eyes just traced the sparkle of a jump of matter left and right
Then slowed to rest once more within the wood, away from prying eye
"Oh ef, you've hid the bell again from me? who knows, so why so sly?"

"Perhaps too much already done and said, well only time will tell
You know my reasons, from another, guides my actions t'ward the bell
Love in light as actuation, quench the soul's desire for love
Only natural laws have weight, reflected here as from above"

"For like all others do i follow intuition as my guide
Whispered words of truth and love spawn forth with no desire to hide
Never will there be a secret, words unspoken to a bean
As desired by creation, finding union, all is seen"

"For who's to say where lovers rest until they meet one fateful day
When souls can merge, becoming one, unlimited, becomes the play
Yet ever present in the heart, *the choice* resides 'tis true
To wipe away confusion and regain the clearest view"

Elder flower walked away, inspired by love so pure and true
His final words slipped through a whisper, there, imagination grew
Strawberry angel smiled and sighed, for undisclosed his purpose was
Such a tricky situation, just as if were penned by Boz

So on with words to paint the pictures, all the moments viewed as life
Time for reference, see the changing, learn from error, veer from strife
Wander where the mirror beckons, see it beckon unto thee
Time to wipe away confusion, time perhaps for *you to see*

~*~

8

The seeds were sown, desires so strong, within the heart and mind of bean
The time was right, the light it grew, within the place that is unseen
O'er several years of unknown pace, each step towards the light it grew
'Tis so for every bean; you see? *a single choice* and one so true

'Tis hard for some to understand the way the mind can simply change
All based on will, a heart's desire, in truth there's nothing out of range
Or how a frame of mind can change, all truth before it then to see
No judgement then, just understanding, knowing's part of being free

The *fast* did slow the body's feeds, understanding all the needs
Consciously to choose the path, always how we sow the seeds
As oneness beckons unto thee, no need to see the wraith
Patience, love, and always trust, forever building faith

The bean, with faith, endured the days and every night his love it grew
Within his dreams he played the game, enchanted by the strand so new
Before him was a path laid out, guided now with strand in hand
Once a hill was now a mountain, there, atop the promised land

The rainbow mountain colour base, as plain a red could be
Here begins the balancing, the energies, you see
Then on to orange, yellow, green, communicating blue
It seems within each band of light, there's different things to do

With indigo illuminated, sight becomes so true
To indicate a helpless state, the carnal force in me and you
Angelic forces serve you dear, if only, you, their voice could hear
Fast the earth, the air, the water, fire's a voice as nature's daughter

Twas in a dream so deep and true, did he first catch a glimpse of you
A heart's desire, a prayer, a song, a road that isn't short or long
Incarnate here, then pass and sing, and back again as though in ring
To learn specifics as your choice, learning purpose, hear your voice

He balanced then, each colour true, the perfect shade, the perfect hue
Slowly, softly, step by step, he marked the plan with time
From in the darkness came a light, the expectation was sublime
So quiet as in whisper, placed a love divine in thee,
The voice, the one creator, reached within and joined the tree

Red, the colour of the land, 'twas dry and dusty in his hand
Before him like a blood-soaked sand, the work of mother nature's hand
The riddle in his *other* hand, a seed of truth, of love and light
The question of his place to stand, a judge and jury of his sight

As preparation for the journey, feeling tired, thirsty too,
Plant the seed and share the water, keep it pure and flowing true
Honouring of mother nature, sharing with me all her flesh
See divine this very fabric, see the matrix, see the mesh

The seed as sown, it then was watered, life created there anew
Know thy place, a true creator, share the love and see the *you*
Waters flowing, love divine, eternal truth within a rhyme
Roots are set, the growth begins, mind the pace and watch the time

A mild rumble o'er the land, before him, mother nature's grand
The roots they grew so big and true, they laid a solid path for you
To keep you safe and clear of dust, of wasted time expressed as rust
For when you choose as choose you can, to be much more than woo or man

And seek to hear a higher you, the timing's always right and true
You just decide that you will see, the simple truth to set you free
Up the mountain, through the bands, bouncing over coloured lands
A goal, a destination set, like milk and honey, near the net

~*~

9

Elder flower came back and shuddered as the mild rumble echoed
Through the multiverse dimensions, and the energy was balanced
Strawberry angel blinked three times and echoed in awareness
(A blur through space/time, yes, without a certain apprehension
What seemed a simple transportation, conjured to deceive the eye)

"There, it has begun", he said, he paused and then he spun her round
Spun her gently round again, to blur the vision of the ground
Strawberry angel felt no vibe from ground to air, no not the same
She looked from tree to ef and back, and as she spun a third
It seemed that she was now alone, and ef was now a bird

It flew up high beyond the cloud, beyond where eye could see
And there the senses grew and wondered, all the same, as plain it be
Back on ground the strawberry angel saw one of her friends go by
Twas daisy fairy, "hey", she called her, close to whisper, winked her eye

"I've a chance, a chance to breathe i have, and need it, do i true
It's like a blur, yet full it was, and secrets do i hold so dear
I feel like i'm just gabbling on, my mind is all askew
I have to share this secret now, else i'll forget, i fear"

"What secret's that then?" daisy asked, began to look about
"For secrets come round quietly, though everyone would love to shout"
"I have a secret, maybe more, but only time will tell
A myth, do you remember of the teaching of the bell?"

"The bell" said daisy fairy, "of the fairy bell, you say
These aren't such things to talk of lightly, in some jest or part of game
Here you talk of things considered, part of life, of breath itself
Guard your words sweat strawberry angel, mind who gathers round in
stealth"

"Were it not so crazy special, were it not so super true
I'd not share this with another, 'cept perhaps a friend like you
Such a secret does i carry, daisy, it is such a burden
Though i feel the sense of drama, i'll not panic, how absurdum"

"Elder flower came to me and showed me where the bell was hid
He spoke of love, of fate, of truth and of another, so he did
There's things occurring, change is due, this is the truth i share with you
A journey soon i will begin, my heart begins to grow anew"

Strawberry angel's eyes weren't seeing, forming pictures of a lover
Heart now fired up by magic, surely there could be no other
Isn't this the point of life, to find the perfect love for thee?
Instead of trying to find the answer, found in depths, of root of tree?

Daisy fairy felt a hole begin to grow inside her being
Thoughts of love weren't on her mind and happy scenes she wasn't seeing
"Why d'you have to be this way, with all things special just for you
The sweetest smile, the brightest wings, a giving heart, a shiny shoe"

"What of me then, strawberry angel, thoughts of me? i'm thinking not
Where's his mate? a date; a four-some, such a giving heart? what rot"
"Daisy fairy that's not me, love isn't pollen on a tree
Love's a single seed of truth that's found in mind and held in youth"

They briefly came together, will they part, perhaps no more to say?
Strawberry angel paused in fancy, daisy yearned to walk away
Clinging tight to gloom and doom, for her it seems there was no room
For truth and love to fill her mind, not everyone is so inclined
Her mutterings were constant, as her strength to drag the negative
It acted like a sedative, to dimly light her way

~*~

10

Deep beneath the surface of the ground, the mole he stood
He felt the rumble in the dirt, in different ways no others could
He felt much more than simple vibes, he felt the life, the very pulse
Specific wave, so deep in colour, rich in hue, without convulse

The steady ripple, balance found, was like a message through the ground
It wasn't just a change you see, there's more to meet the I in thee
So, at a junction underground, he paused to feel, to sense, to know
Then had a message, new, just found, and must deliver it to foe

This little junction underground, where many tunnels meet
The knowing mole did spin about, awareness then, complete
Part of his choices, as in life, is seen, he chose a different path
At certain moments, fast included, deep inside with help from garth

On and upwards through the tunnels, coming out just near the pub
Over which an office stood, the occupant enjoyed the grub
In the evening darkness, all the lights were bright and cheery
Could never find a reason why, so no one sought a theory

The truth of course, not known by many, not admitted to, 'tis true
That someone always funds the others, out to search for you know who
Not for him, he's there, we know, but bits of stuff, a nod and whisper
Idle gossip, have a care, you'll find yourself stuck in the crisper

~*~

11

Twas all at once, like time stood still, the fairy breath sucked in with fear
To hear the voice and not to know, when merddyn speaks, a light to grow
The wise would listen, would not speak, an insight here and you can peak
A gift for sure for all to see, yet none to witness this with thee

For players are, as parts are cast, a choice abounds from first to last
Like unto blur and mist and breeze, a merddyn walks with you at ease
In the shadows, in the light, plain to see and out of sight
There's a knowing in your heart, hear the voice and let it start
All can come and all can see, the light inside to set you free

Each a piece upon a board, to learn of life and love and light
No exceptions to the *word*, affected all, we have no plight
Guided with a knowing hand, the voice to steel a thousand souls
Fearless, faithful, knowing, true, accepting of the choice in roles

Feel the power, see the force, the energy 'tis here
Conjured by a master hand, the evidence is clear
Others then, there is a knowing, feel the coming o'er the land
Loving sage, a timeless walker, always then, as always planned

"Harken unto me young daisy, listen strawberry angel do"
The voice was unmistakeable, like all the things it always knew
The voice did not induce a fear, though danger's never far away
Expressing his concerns, he was, and sowed the seed, as of his play

"Mind your business, guard it true and therein lies the task for you
Each a story here to learn, error/truth, one can discern
Step by step a path to take, choose with love, make no mistake
You made mention of the bell, but what's now gone you cannot tell"

("Gone!") shrieked daisy in her mind and not a word was heard
("There's magic here, an ancient force, a magic undeterred")
"Merddyn, oh my lord, who called you?" strawberry angel cried in fear
"Who would need your ancient forces, who would want to feel you near?"

"Silence now!" did merddyn roar, then soften down to velvet floor
With dulcet tones and words of love, he handled each as though in glove
Motionless the fairies were, the eyes moved first, then head when tied
The blur of motions chased the voice, just as the movements so implied

Each would slowly spin; a simple turn as though were tied to ground
His voice demanding focus, that of purpose; chosen gathered round
"I heard a whisper, not a shout mind, someone up on silbury hill
Prepped some land for something special, someone's heart, a dream to fill"

"There's a trek, a journey true, if it's a love that captures you
I've a sense no sense can see, how such a love can work on thee
The roots stretch under all the land, connected with the same
A lover's knot entwined on fate? the strangest question bolts the gate
A gossip's tongue, it can bestrew all types of stuff, a wicked brew
A gossip's words will enter one, to talk beyond the setting sun"

A glimpse, a flash of merddyn's robe, slips in and out of folds in time
To see a change, to hear anew, surrenders to a path sublime
As quickly as he came he went, as always just enough is said
To sow the seeds of fate and love, always choices, paths to tread

Strawberry angel, darling fairy, spinning slowly in the air
There about her, daisy fairy, neither really seemed aware
Each looked at the other, blinked a lot and gasped out loud
Things like this don't happen often, never draw a crowd

"That was merddyn", daisy whispered, "came for us, i tell you true
Quiet words and weaving magic, there's a path laid out for you
In your dreams you'll soon discover all the new you can embrace
Feel the pressure, on a timeline, strawberry, you've to run a race"

"I must go and find my centre, you must go and seek to rest
Have no fear my darling sister, you will always do your best
I'm not angry; feeling, knowing, that this time has come for thee
As is chosen, so will fruit, to cast thy future on the sea"

Daisy hastily departed with a mark as black as night
A scar of old is seen to splinter, here it seems, the cause of fright
Days of old, dark days remembered, history poisons present love
All is but her mind's creation, blinded not from light above

Off it seems to drown her sorrows, drown herself within the drink
There a jealous rage develops, fuelled by madness, on the brink
Many there to goad and worry, turn the key and wind her up
Then down and down into her sorrows, here's another, drink it up

Strawberry angel, darling fairy, simply sits to take it in,
To try and slow a mind that's racing, all that happened, all the din
"Surely there must be a reason, why the strangest things occur
Maybe i should just embrace them with a smile; hello, bonjour"

Softly did she float away, so gently, bouncing through a dream
"He spoke of love, he spoke of fate, it sounds so charming, so serene
Is this a special moment? yes, a special one he said!
However will i find my rest, i have no use a bed"

"I'm all a *blubble*, *splib* and *pibble*, see, love grows inside of me!"
"Sounds like indigestion, 'course you could be going gaga
Which might only rhyme with *baba*", said a rat sat up a tree

"Oh roy, d'you really think so? this is such a special day
I mean, not saying that i'm special, but i kinda had a feeling
That things just, might go my way"

"Listen, i saw everything, it really looked fantastic
You two caught in swirling winds
With flashes true of merddyn's cloak

Not flashes then of lightning
No, not a drop of rain to soak"

"And yes, he spoke of love, it's true, and maybe that's the path for you?"
Roy the rat came down to ground and slowly turned to run away
But paused and turned to strawberry angel, "love and light on you this day
Sleep sweet strawberry angel do, there's visions there to steal for you"

Darling strawberry angel paused and watched him slip away
'So stealthy with his measured step to always calculate his day
A friend indeed and always true, his thought and words to comfort you
Now on to home to find my bed, to try and rest my weary head'

~*~

12

Hours later, daisy spills the secrets in the pub,
Von stroodle needs no magic lantern when you drink without the grub
"It's true I tell you", daisy howled, "there's magic in the air this night
'Tis strawberry angel's time he said, he'd seen her do these things alright"

The pub was full, a motley crew, and all employed by you know who
As innocent as some might feel, your soul, for favour, they would steal
Like berti' badger, news reporter, glandwey goblin and her dogs
And all the others sitting, drinking local beer from hollowed logs

They listened hard to daisy's tale, then laughed and howled, she seemed so
lost
Envy is a wicked master, always time to pay the cost
They goaded her, was wound up tight, the tears burst forth from out the sight
Her stomach tight, her heart broke too, whatever was a girl to do?

The howling's and the laughter travelled up the stairs into an ear
An ear of someone caught in thought of what he might acquire with fear
An ancient longing in his heart to see as beans do see
To skip a step, in gods own plan and now embrace what sets you free

His empire was enormous when you think of all he had
The pub, the news, the health club, well not everything was bad
So many thoughts beyond his form, from hat through suit to boot
More wisdom than the owl perhaps, but who would give a hoot

Still, things he knew and secrets hid, just like all beans of old
So self-serving, full of fear, with secrets never told
Heard the tale of timely cycles, how the cycles fill our mind
Love and light to change the form, to walk as cured, no longer blind

Down the stairs he walked so slowly from his office overhead
Daisy squawked, while others silenced voice, as hearts did fill with dread
Slowly walking to the singer, solo singer in our midst
Tempted then to bash the table, mark the presence with a fist

Instead, with forethought, and with will imparted true; a warmth within?
And sat before young daisy fairy, flashing his sincerest grin
"Oh daisy, darling fairy, oh so beautiful you are,
A privilege to sit before you, see you drink the beer in jar"

"For you no sorrows shall you see nor tempers will you waste
Come barman fill her glass with gin, to drink is no disgrace"
As ordered, so he did obey, then daisy drank it down
Twas filled again to ease her plight or loosen tongue beneath the frown

"What troubles thee young daisy fairy, tell me, tell me truly do
For I have all the time for thee, so ease your pain and drink the brew"
All around were eyes of terror, eyes of fear of those that knew
The madness in his method, and this fairy who he would subdue

"Tell me daisy, tell me all that lurks within your darkened heart,
Don't let a hatred slip away, embed it fully at the start
Nurture it with drink and love, three spoons of pity, dark above
All negativities a feast, then all your life just feed the beast"

"Leave me be", young daisy wailed, "again i'm second, loved i'm not
That merddyn said it, sod I say, 'tis like he said, for change I pray
But no, it's her, that strawberry angel, there I said it", gasps were heard
A moment's rest, then all about, when all did jeer and laugh and shout

"And yes, it was that daisy fairy, silly daisy fairy, who was heard,
To say she loves the little strawberry angel fairy, really? how absurd... "
A deathly silence filled the room, he finished word and then did swoon
As though to bite her throat clean through, for him it's not so hard to do

Von stroodle is a guinea pig, a mind of evil discontentment
He controlled the very room, yes, every thought and every sentiment
Then out the corner of his eye, 'twas morris mole, unlikely spy
He slowly walked to base of stairs, von stroodle winked, seemed unawares
All others truly were the stars, von stroodle was in daisy's jar
The pain so easily did grow, and daisy chose to drink from sorrow

"Hollow, hollow, loveless land of sadness and despair,
Distraught i am, my heart feels blackened; listen all and have a care"
"But where's she going?", shrieked von stroodle, making everybody jump
Almost like he didn't care, thought "what-ever!" not a grump

Daisy found herself relaxing, "seeing as he doesn't care
Why should i care myself at all, care about her silly hair
She always seems to get her way, she's going now, hip hip hooray!
Up silbury hill to find her love, guided by a hand above"

Her eyes began to fill with tears, and slowly rolled their way down face
Building with her sadness true, was now a feeling of disgrace
Of letting down a loving friend, "sweet strawberry angel, loves i do
My sister sweet, she knows it, true"

And there and then poor daisy rested, head on arms and fell to sleep
Von stroodle smiled and all attested, all her secrets his to keep
"So strawberry's for a walk up silbury, up to silbury? is it true?
I wonder, what might be the reason, finding love? that's something new!"

"We know young strawberry angel loves; it seems like none of us know how
All living creatures, forms of life, from smallest bug to biggest cow
Is that enough, an indication of a heart that's true and full
Influenced by moon and cycles, can she feel it, feel the pull?"

Von stroodle turned, he spun away, a nod, a wink, he scanned the room
"Eyes and ears then, keep 'em keen", and pondered more on strawberry's doom
As he and mole went up the stairs to talk in quiet of things surreal
Of love and light and journeys bold, there is no sense, and yet we feel

No words were said, as stairs they climbed, on landing walked to office door
A morris paused there at the doorway, waiting for von stroodle's paw
Klaus opened door, bade morris enter, morris did and walked to chair
Each enjoyed this genteel moment, seemed relaxed, without a care

"Well hello, morris, nice to see you, confidante and special friend
Have you come to bring me news that just might send me round the bend?"
"News that might just send you giddy", morris spoke and flashed a grin
"I felt it, like you said i would, a certain vibe, a certain din"

Both sat down as suzy entered, suzy mouse, with tea and cake
For just a moment, not a whisper, keeping secrets, no mistake
Each hesitated, waiting moments, hear the footsteps lead away
Down the stairs to all and sundry, have a drink enjoy yer stay

"She's gone", von stroodle winked at morris, "let me have it, tell me all
Was it as we both expected, are we on-track overall?"
Morris smiled a little smile, a tiny nod, a wink, was true
"Indeed we are, least as i think it, i'll explain, it's up to you"

"I tunnelled under solsbury hill just as you asked that i should do
And listened out for things i felt, all very strange, and colours too
And there the strangest thing occurred, and yes, it took me by surprise
I felt a difference, then a hue, i felt the red, i tell no lies"

"Go on", he said, "i doubt thee not most trusted and most loyal friend"
Von stroodle offered morris cake, "...'twas then, just as i round the bend
The last i'd dug, cut clean it was, the walls so smooth to carry sound
As far as anyone could see, to hear all noises underground"

"I thought i heard a voice i did, all faint, i felt it *old*
It tickled hairs upon my neck, these sounds weren't of a normal mould
I hung around for several hours, I felt that there was more to come
And sure enough it hit me, but there was no sound, no words were sung"

"I closed my eyes to focus hard, yet slipped into a restful dream
With all things coloured, red in hue, a lake was fed by flowing steam
Each thought i had, the surface waters of the lake did bounce and dance
Instinctively i sought to calm these troubled waters while in trance"

"I felt it red, i saw it too, is this the information sought?
I hope i haven't wasted time, to make us both end up distraught
"No – no", von stroodle drank some tea and motioned him to carry on
"This really is a revelation, one could say its sine qua non "

"There isn't that much more to tell, the feelings and the sound, the hue
The *ages* in the distant voice, not heard before, and so was new"
"The voice was old you said before, the voice, the sound of elder flower
Not dissimilar perhaps, a certain charm, a hint of power?"

"Now you come to mention it, there's not much difference 'tween the two
Von stroodle, i salute you sir, you clever thing, i'd not a clue"
Von stroodle's finger tapped his nose, "a secret now, no more to tell,
How does this fit with strawberry angel and the sacred fairy bell?"

~*~

13

The bean had fed, as though on fast, and soon would lay his head to sleep
He felt the change, the change for good, the balanced red for him to keep
He planned the harmonies in mind and saw the fields, the fiery hue
He found his love was good and kind, and fired his passion bold and new

His many meditations and the focus on the same
The seeker and the calling, it's a most important game
The mother bean gave total space, to let the young bean learn and grow
Questions, answers, both within, just tend your heart, then you will know

The bean would sit in observation, looking on at every thing
The life that took its toll in making, psychometric visions sing
To smell the earth in such a way, to know its presence deep inside
A sense that it's a part of thee, a vehicle then, and always tied

So much becomes much less a blur, no need the gold, the scent, the myrrh
So much becomes so clear for you, when you just change the things you view
His heart was set on love divine, existing then, in total bliss
The purest love, a choice of mine, like pausing during love's first kiss

Supported by a sight so rare that only comes with time and love
The earthly parents guiding hand, expressions then, of god above
The greatest gift or work to do, to be of service then, for you,
And you for them, and them for them, perhaps we'll *ad infinitum*

Each trip around the inner ring, illusions then, created out
And so, in life we dance and sing and sometimes shake it all about
But all is choice, a choice for you, if you would dare to be so bold
So take control of only you, the same was said in days of old

The bean stepped slowly down the stairs and followed light inside the room
So strong the vibes within this house, so full of love and never doom
Gladys lived inside this house, a friend to all when time was right
A synchronous connection found, when needed, for both day or night

"Evening teddy, getting late now, how's my little man tonight
Walking through the coloured bands? i think the moon is out tonight.
Ooh, i'm sensing balanced nature, red in hue, you've got control"
Teddy smiled inside just knowing, avoiding race, embracing stroll

"What was that?" asked gladys from the kitchen,
"D'you just say he's done the red? this time round he's reaching higher
It's ten o'clock, should be in bed"

Teddy's mum, whose name was zo, stood up to greet her only son
Her take on life was quite unique, she only entertained the fun
The sad, the dour, the guilty too, can all just go, i tell you true

"I'm full of beans", young teddy said, as gladys came into the room
"It's pointless going up to bed, no fresh air there, more like a tomb
Perhaps i'll sit out back a while and search the sky for brightest love
There's little cloud, a gentle breeze, it's not that cold, no need for glove"

From gladys, teddy got a hug, and "love him" were the words she spoke
Next came mum, a warm embrace, in her this did a smile invoke
"Off you go then, wrap up warm and don't be out too long"
It's déjà vu, for all of us, a common mother's song

Teddy went about his way, the ladies smiled and watched him on
In admiration of his passion; knew it wouldn't be that long
Each a chosen role to play, as part of theirs, to make and choose
Co-creating merging minds, only service, never ruse

"I felt him here", old gladys said, "last night and then this afternoon
His eyes upon us from the hill, and then within young teddy's room
He found him out and judged him true, he's here to help, of course he knew
No interference must we make, avoiding then a grave mistake"

Her voice was different, back it changed, "kettle on, a sleepy brew?
Good to get a good night's sleep, perhaps some chamomile for you"
Gladys, she was such a treasure, treasure yes, to one and all
Her life she saw as such a pleasure, every day she had a ball

Zo looked on, "sounds good to me, it's such a pleasure, herbal tea
I feel a presence close by too, the owl on hill has splendid view!"
Gladys nodded, smiled, and stirred the cup of tea, though thought of bird
"He slips through nature, time and space, to see each bean complete the race"

"Success,
Through dedication,
In all innocence", said the bean

Be confident, in the innocence of awareness in experience
This - is the faith - that replaces - all fear

Just seek to be close to the one who's all loving
Work hard on your task, as the changes draw near

"Be all loving"

~*~

14

The very morning following the day of those beginnings
Saw strawberry angel, darling fairy, feeling not amused
It seemed her head was all befuddled, full of ooey gooey fillings
Lovey dovey nonsense then, and all her thoughts appeared confused

"It does make sense! i know, i heard it; saw him and her, moved i was
Said i'd lover's work before me, was this wizard up from oz?
A so-called secret, then there's daisy, what if she to all would tell?
Best i go and check this secret, find again the sacred bell"

Strawberry angel, darling fairy, set off down a path to dingle
There she hoped to find her prize, excitement grew and made her tingle
She skipped and jumped and flew so high, she never would see spying eye
So carried care-free on her way and dreamed how love might come to stay

The clouds were out, the sky was blue, 'twas such a simple thing to do
Here in mother nature's arms, another perfect day to view
A momentary gust of wind caressed the fairy on her cheek
Riding thermals in and out of clouds to take a peek

Twas freddy f the peregrine, majestic up above
Von stroodle's eye to cover miles in between the meals of dove
Freddy flew as fast as night or hovered high to see it all
Every day was full of fun, life was easy, life's a ball

He watched her skip from tree to tree, as on to bell her heart did race
Yet all her moves were nonchalant, no stress or tension in her pace
It seems young strawberry angel knew just when to rush and when to not
"Loose lips Lil, what me? don't think so; need to find more on this plot"

Slowly there with caution, not with stealth, but with a care
Young strawberry angel, darling fairy, used her smarts i do declare
Inside her head she talked and whispered 'bout a love for her so true
Pretty sneaky, strawberry angel, *not so much* the ingénue

Finally, upon the space where tree doth stand and bell resides
Not there on show for all to see, but based on fear a secret hides
She searched around the base of tree, a pocket yet to find
Where one could hide a sacred bell, there hidden from the blind

Around and then around again and then around once more
"This isn't right, it cannot be, no pocket full, no secret door
This is the tree, i know it so, it's... wait a minute, magic winks it's eye at me
But i've a mind to walk away, forget the plot, ignore the plea"

A crash of thunder, clouds of darkness, stirring up all o'er the head
Hold there steady, mind thy wits, one fateful move, you could be dead
"Hold on fear, imagination! thoughts are not to be believed
Find the faith, renew the passion, walk the tapestry as weaved"

And there and then the voice of merddyn sent cold shivers down her spine
Transfixed her form and caught her breath, "behold a path of golden twine
Understand the guidance here, for everyone it's all the same
Tip toe gently through your life, for life is just a simple game"

Strawberry angel's eyes grew wide as merddyn's form revealed him here
Down from up above flew freddy, getting closer, sure to hear
There upon a branch, with talons fixed to hold him true
He watched bewitched with magic works, indeed, just as we always do

Twas then the apparition formed and so became the man
Artful in his timeless being, limitless for all he can
He leaned upon his staff of life, a jewel of white atop the crown
Then pulled *love's arrow*, out from hiding, underneath his dark blue gown

"Mark thee well young strawberry angel, catch these words I spin for thee
Seek the fateful balance in the choices that you'll surely see
You've a task and task it is, yet always choice will sing for all
A choice to open up your heart and guide yourself, your youth enthral"

Fixed and fastened on the spot, strawberry angel just observed
Her eyes so wide, her heart just pounds, such moments do for all subserve
Merddyn took *love's arrow,* bright white light, and fashioned it in size
It shrunk in length to that of finger right before her very eyes

Laying there upon his palm, he gently blew *love's arrow* pure
"With this, the divine compass, any seeker's now a connoisseur"
It spun away to strawberry angel, sat it did upon her hand
"Keep it safe within your pocket, safe from all - please understand"

Merddyn emphasised importance just as anyone could see
Strawberry angel simply nodded, gulped, and stuck like glue to tree
"What about the bell, it's missing, looked i did; the bell it's gone"
"Never mind the bell young strawberry, you're to sing a different song"

"There atop o' silbury hill, the bell will sit and wait for thee,
But know the danger in each step, as others wish the light to see
Mark each zig and zag with caution, all your journey have a care
To err, divine forgiveness giving, find the passion! will you dare?"

"There's another, seeks with such frustrated desperation
The timelessness of passing moments, thoughts of doubt forever played
Avoid the wagging tongues, so mean, the hand that seeks a grand occasion
Often seems to lose control, the weight with which each movement's made"

"Know that every step you take, the hand will seek to cut you down
The madness will consume them all, confusion's veil becomes a gown
Careful then, your tailor's cloth, for all that you would see as real
Is all that you will ever find, you choose the package and the deal"

With but a breath, the shape was gone and all the air could capture not
The moment in the frame of time that hinted of a greater plot
Strawberry angel breathed as words and pictures flashed across her mind
With presence did she ease emotion, halt all fantasy unkind

Self-control would keep her strong, help her focus, clear the sight
No more would she seek in error, have no fear in dark of night
Accepting everything encountered, consequence of steps we take
Yes, it seems the bell has gone, that's the plan, and no mistake

With things, they're just the way they are, and that's the way they seem to me
Exactly as we chose, else they'd be different, don't you see?
Sometimes too much detail takes up time, we found a great distraction
Leads us on our way to other thoughts, and then to pointless action

Her head was once again found spinning, focus on specific words
Don't waste time on flights of fancy, fact not fiction! how absurd
"Home to rest, then off tomorrow, up the top of silbury hill
Don't know why i need the compass, each mistake could be a thrill"

Strawberry angel had a plan, well least a goal, or so it seemed
More a job, a task, a chore, well, not so much; in love it's themed
She gave herself a little smile, as off to home she flew on cruise
And then she had a scary thought: "this love of mine i cannot choose?"

"What if there is no appeal, no fancy or desire
But this is magic, this is fate, i'll not be stepping deep in mire"
Strawberry carried on her way as freddy falcon took to air
He'd seen and heard the details, but for random thoughts he had no care

He watched her for a moment as towards her home she surely flew
Then turned to go see klaus von stroodle, here's a guy he clearly knew
Would pay him well for information, with perhaps a dove or two
Remembering the taste and flavour, so his power and speed it grew

Distracted by a flash of light, the white of dove, the flesh, the life
The plight of one who's fate is sealed, the final pain, the final strife
He found a perch to rest a while, his belly full, no empty plate
And with regard the latest news, it seems poor klaus would have to wait

~*~

15

The morning then, at base of mound, the bean outside, at peace was found
The fast was long, the journey short, no time to sing or here cavort
The mind in focus, sure to see, illumination come in thee
The astral form did slip to view, the inside out, well, what a view!

Twas now that he could dance and sing like never as before
Or float up through the ceiling, yes, or even through a door
No 'thing' on earth could stop him as he flew from tree to tree
Then stopped to look at bertimus who's looking back at he

"Can you see me mr badger?" asked the bean in astral form
"Yes", the badger answered slowly, "though it doesn't seem the norm
Normally you seem more pasty, whingey, whiney, squeaky voice
You sort of seem more real i s'pose, does every bean here have this choice?"

The bean, he smiled a knowing smile and asked the badger of his way
What brought him here to this fair garden, what's he searching for today
"Well i guess it's information, 'bout the fairy and the bell
The fairy bell that's missing? I guess no one's here to you to tell?"
"To tell to me, no, no one, true, is this a thing that you would do?"

"It wasn't me, not bertimus the badger, don't you see?
I just report the news, i write it down as plain can be
So this is what occurred, i tell you straight and this is so
Official gossip, that's the press, we have our place you know"

"Twas guinea pig that told me, klaus von stroodle owns the lot
'Bert', he said, 'a word, a secret's out i kid you not'
Can't forget the image of the moment on that day
Twas first i heard the whisper that the whisper's come to play

'Bert', he said, 'i've just a whisper, need to check it out
Need you on yer toes 'ere mate, keep it quiet, never shout
Merddyn saw a clearing, 'twas a breaking in the fog
He saw a boy awaken, should be sleeping like a log'"

"'Ask about, cos things they change, they never stay the same
You know the things you're looking for, the nature of our game'
A finger shot up to my brow, a nod, a click, a wink
'Got the picture chief', i said, 'a newsflash on the brink'"

"I walked out of his office as it sat above the pub
I'd had a beer there earlier as i shovelled down me grub
We heard the things that daisy said and then he called us round
To go and search for all the info, all that lays upon the ground"

"And so, i ask about a bit and then i ask some more
I find most people helpful as they show me out the door
Twas smarty pants the rat, um, roy? knew what was going on
He seemed to know it all he said, but only sang in song

"'You should go see elder flower, elder flower, elder flower
You should go see elder flower, who wants another pot
Ask him what he wants it for, wants it for, wants it for
Ask him what he wants it for, and what's the lovers' knot?'"

"So, i sought out old elder flower, a friend of merddyn true
To find out what the whisper was and other things he knew
He grew a little curly smile, content that i was there
He muttered little bits of words that vanished in the air

"'You want to know what's up', he asked, 'and if there's something wrong?
You ask of fear and panic, is it heaving in the throng?
While most can give no answer save for smarty pants the rat
It seems you found your way to me, for that i tip my hat'"

"'Tis true i need a pot for gold as simple as it's true
For i have seen a heart that's pure, and yes, the owner knew
Of how he might secure the love divine we yearn to see
So i've a task to help and guide, just as i would with thee'"

"'Merddyn has performed a spell, a prayer and picture forms
We have to keep things under wraps we can't afford no storms
If this gets out, acidic things will cling to all that's good
Old al k'line's a friend, you know? so take his help we should'"

"I've never heard of al k'line, no, never heard that name
But keep in the back of mind that magic's in this game
Elder flower's sort of strange, and some might say he's weird
And merddyn's back, I kid you not, now he's the one that's feared"

"Why's he feared"? the young bean asked, "what d'e do to you?"
"Well nothing", bertimus replied, "you saying it isn't true"?
"A fear has permeated time, of course it could be lies
All truth is individual"; the bean not finished, no replies

"By the way, my name, it's 'al', that's 'al k'line', i know, it's true
It's weird, it's synchronous of course, we're finding things we're meant to do
Like meeting here and chatting now, about the things now going on
Like how a pig called klaus von stroodle wants to sing a different song"

"Do you live here, um, are you new, can't say i've seen you here before
What d'you do, d'you know you're fading, what you doing off the floor?"
"You see a different type of me that's also me, look over there"
He pointed to himself of course, his olive skin, his dark brown hair

"I walk here three or four times daily, out and back then out again
Labour loves a choice in freedom, can't say every trip's the same
The goal's the top, all infinite, to find the clearest view
I seek to find a union, after which i'll savour life anew"

Bertimus went on to talk of all the things he thought he knew
Of daisy blabbing all that stuff, 'bout strawberry, "oh yes that was true,
There's magic here, make no mistake, and merddyn walks this very land
Some say he's here to aid another, making sure all goes as planned"

"I've seen no warlock", bean replied, "and no idea how one would seem?
Both in and out of time and space? it sounds amazing, makes me keen
To meet this sorcerer supreme, this man of old whose life is guile
Who sees the truth in all our ways, who seeks to lend us all a style"

Bean and badger parted, badger going back towards the pub
Von stroodle isn't mean you know, his people get free beer and grub
Back to hear of progress and report on all that one has seen
To help, to force the hand of nature, klaus von stroodle has a dream

Al k'line, the bean, the boy, continued on in astral form
Yet again discovering a way of talk that is the norm
To animals, without the fear that's felt when beans are drawing near
Place the trust inside the mind, to know the bean that's always kind

The bean progressed in orange, knowing who the badger meant to tell
Empathy, compassion felt, no scraps of anger found to swell
It tasted right to 'al' the bean, who then saw yellow coming on
Felt the presence, in awareness, saw the choices in the song

Step by step, each colour found, to find the balance through the trust
The balance, it is so important, for your progress it's a must
Sit within each colour found, and answer all the questions true
Seek the truth within thy self, understand the fool in you

~*~

16

Twas later on that afternoon, saw strawberry angel on her way
All there was, was silbury hill, no silken thread her path to lay
So taken was she with the thought of finding love and love alone
With nothing more than hope in heart, she left the safety of her home

'Tis true she knew of silbury hill and of the bearing she should tread
The top, the goal, the heart drives on, inside the mind prepares the bed
All she could remember was the warning of a wood
Of evil lurking deep inside, how entering, it served no good

The sun still out and overhead, she reached the edge of village wall
And there beyond protective gates, the rolling hills not city sprawl
She paused and turned and caught her breath, as though to say goodbye
But none were there to see her off, no tear to wipe from eye

She thought of daisy, angry, sad, bad tempered, feeling blue
She judged her not, but loved her more, because she simply *knew*
The power of love is giving in to all the catalysts we meet
Forgiveness is a powerful tool to help the freedom feel complete

Merddyn's artful sowing saw awareness grow inside her head
This is a way that things are seen, to nudge all seekers on their way
Words can form, electric sparks, can come as dreams inside your head
Or flash across the light of mind, an insight finds more room to play

She turned and carried on her way, no friend or foe to mark her time
So not with haste, but careful step, for soon she'll have a hill to climb
Along the road until we find the crossing and another path
Turn through choice, seek new awareness, grow in love, more time to laugh

Choices, choices all the time, to think, to say, to really do
Co-creation every moment, in your mind you see it too
Things you want, imagination, expectation draws it near
Co-create the real, the present, you'll get yours so have no fear

Strawberry angel, darling fairy, on a quest, a quest for love
In her heart she feels a blessing from the one who's seen above
The truth of course, is that the form of god is in all things we know
The works are so extensive, even in the mirror he will show

Strawberry hadn't thought of time or just how long this quest might take
She felt the course of action, true and certain, it was no mistake
She followed on along the path alone, it seems the only way,
The earth continues spinning round, her task will not complete this day

When in a clearing she could see the top of silbury, green and blue
Not that many clouds around to spoil an almost perfect view
She smiled and glowed with warmth inside, here in mother nature's arms
Who builds our flesh and air to breath, enticing all with all her charms

On and over ditch and stream, through bush and meadow, gentle brook
Every now and then consider, change direction? pause and look
Strawberry didn't know this place, had not been here before
Flew straight across the red bank valley, waste of time to trace the floor

The orange grove was full of blossom, oils to make a cake taste sweet
On to lemons, yellow pure, to see them all was such a treat
Soon the sun would start to dip, beyond the crest of hill in view
Maybe time to test the theory, check direction, find it new

Out the glowing arrow came and gently laid upon her hand
Inside her head she saw it sparkle, start to rise as though were planned
So it followed in her palm, she co-created, proved it true
Arrow rose into position, as expected it would do

She shook her head and carried on, ignoring what the arrow said
She must go straight, no time to spare, now thinking of her cosy bed
This little detour that she took, this forest thickens, is she lost?
The light, it fades, how soon the night? will she be out for morning frost?

The arrow showed a safest way to reach the place that must be found
Not so much a direct route, no, more a zig 'n' zag on ground
But strawberry saw a different path, so headstrong could this fairy be
Too often blind to looming danger, what will now become of thee?

While there was sun, late afternoon, the leaves increased to block the light
A darkness growing all around, unaware her growing plight
Strawberry's pace began to slow, the more, about, became surreal
Eerily it crept upon her, cold and menace now to feel

"This is for love", she fed her mind, to find again her heart's desire
She must avoid the searing heat, the doubt, the fear, the greed, the fire
A pace so slow she's never been, a cautious mind on what she's seen
A little house with chimney smoke, be careful, strawberry, else you'll croak

~*~

17

In his office, klaus von stroodle gathered up his wits and plan
He felt the time was getting close, when he would see like woo or man
He cast his mind towards the game, the players known, locations too
and now the brethren gather round, to share the information new

Molly mouse knocked on his door, "come in", he rasped towards the floor
She entered with a cup of tea, a list of names, a biscuit too
"The goblin and her dogs are here, as well the crows, they all are new"
For this, klaus gave an hour no more, "I hope this won't become a bore"

He heaved himself from out of chair, along the floor and out of room
A fairly non-eventful day, not feeling much like va-va-voom
Every month seems much the same, is there really progress here?
Different player, different game, "do i trick myself, i fear"

So easy then for all and any, instantly consumed by doubt
He looked around the floor below, cleared his throat, began to shout
He must, he must, he must press on and never leave the game
This guinea pig is klaus von stroodle, sense the power in the name

"Alright then fellows, listen all, quiet down you over there
I'll share the news to power you on, to help me mind, so have a care
By now you all are most aware of that which daisy chose to share
That dear young strawberry angel's on a quest for love, i do declare"

He grinned and laughed, the show began, he wound them up and flipped them on
He mentioned this and talked of that, he kept control of heaving throng
"And so, there seems to be the two, the two adventures moving on
Strawberry, silbury, bean at solsbury, climbing", there appears a song

"Very strange", von stroodle said, "yes, very strange indeed
Understand this now, we must, if we are to succeed.
We know the boy goes off alone; mysterious for sure!
And strawberry angel makes her way up neighbouring silbury tor"

"Turn that ruddy music off, there's angels all around
Some must get a hold of strawberry, there's a key that must be found
Another group for observation, observation of the bean
Need to blend with all surroundings, in the open never seen"

"Come on, this is hours people, know that i'm not talking days
This is when i need your action, seek my favour, yearn for praise
Here's the rally cry for hunters, gather one and gather all
Find and kill the strawberry angel, steal the arrow, bell 'n' all"

"Freddy, hover over silbury, you can watch out for the bell
Morris, carry on as usual, a certain progress you can tell
Remember all to contact molly, she will keep me up to date
Don't want special information reaching me when it's too late"

"As for keeping eye on bean, we'll use the skills of those that are...
Well, new to us, you understand, we see them here, both near and far
And now with us, this noisy crew? who'd never give you time to doze
A pleasure then, to introduce this happy band, the crooning crows"

"We are the crooning crows, we give an overview
We tell you where to go, but never what to do
And this is how we say we'd like to go along
But everything we say is gonna be in song"

"We..." - "that's enough of that then, ok you sing, i know it's true
But as it hurts my ears, i feel it's time to talk of something new
I wonder then who else will join this little hunting group of mine
So we can get the lamp and compass, find direction, cross the line"

"And so, here is our newest member; foe, not friend, to all the same
Glandwey goblin and her dogs, to kill, for them is just a game
You will search for strawberry angel now she's going up the hill
But wait until she finds the bell, get the compass, then yer kill"

Some inside the room, they shuddered, at the coldness of it all
Blind, unfeeling, that's obsession, running into solid wall
Klaus, through fear and desperation, slipped along to side of knife
Made the ultimate decision, now prepared to take a life

Glandwey goblin, one foot tall, respects no life, but hates it all
Mean and angry all the time, so cold her soul, her heart's in rhyme
See her boots with metal studs to bash an' crush your bones
It seems her mind is now detached, she laughs at any bod' that groans
Dressed in black and brown and blue, for fun she'll take the life from you

Special acorn roller skates, with armour made of bits of shell
Some on her head, her chest, her arse, well, yesterday it seems she fell
Tonight's a night of silver wonder, shinning bright to light the way
"Let's push off an' catch a fairy, she'll not see the light of day"

"Remember glandwey, win my prize and know the wonder that i seek
To kill her now, without the bell, would rob me of that which i speak"
The pig, he turned to stare in eye, "remember when i said she'll die
Only once she has the bell, how many times must thee i tell?"

Klaus, it seemed, was getting mad, his hair was up, he looked real bad
Crazed and blind through blood and guts, there's just one way, there are no buts
With super strength he seemed to fly, from floor to stand upon the bar
It seemed he must reiterate just how they all had come so far

His voice was loud, so strange but true, the evil placed a chill in you
"A warning then to one and all, now heed my words, make sure you know
If either one is seen to fall, then to *your* death, i'll see you go
The only time to kill at all's when bell and compass...

64

Are mine!"

~*~

18

Sophie Alice Daisy Fox was fair of face with strawberry locks
For love she wore awareness true, to win the love of you know who
She too was seeking for a way, to bring together, mind at play
With union of a kind so rare, for those who live without a care

She'd known the bean since she was young,
their mothers being friends an' all
They'd shared their lives, well pretty much,
like Christmas, birthdays parties ball
At special times, on certain days, both came to gladys' and stayed
They learnt to dance, to meditate, cook vegetables, of course they played

She felt the vibes from deep within that emanate from soul
That move in all directions and dimensions every roll
Always nudging, always hinting, seeking *you*, to be aware
Here's a taste, the food of lovers, listen well and have a care

Seekers of illumination, hold on high the hidden ways
Wasting will and faith and love, a lust for power builds a haze
Love illuminates your sight, then all truth in awareness found
This is the knowing, truly, sight and freedom realised on the ground

Imagine truly knowing as the error grew before your eyes
Detached observing, in the moment, full of love, no room for lies
Understand the nature of all gifts, the way all children grow
Simply sow the seeds of love, and there within, the truth to know

Sophie, as a child of god, descends beneath the veil of white
The senses sit 'both' side of knife, confusion found in earthly sight
To each his own, his own it be, now separate the soul in thee
Search for silence deep within, branching out, descend the tree

Her mother was a simple soul whose world was nothing more than paint
"I simply know just who i am and s'pose i know just who i ain't"
She'd found her spot, her groove, her love, all gifted then from up above
The choice was hers, for her to see, "...where happiness was found for me"

Sophie loved her mum, 'Denise', she really wasn't hard to please
Her love was seen to hold no bounds, her voice just full of pleasing sounds
"If you're happy and you're safe, what else is there to be
Unconditionally loving, in your mind completely free?"

There's many ways to find the flame, to find direction, course and pitch
Engaging *will* in co-creation, crawling out the roadside ditch
Thinking, seeing, doing, all the streaming's in awareness new
All the choice is yours, in every co-created thing you do

Sophie wants to be a teacher, be a teacher of the bean
Lives her life as demonstration, truth in all examples seen
Be the truest you can be, to you and all around you find
Love your foe and love yourself, always patient, always kind

Al the bean seems full of wisdom, full of knowing, that's his way
Sophie's 'mother nature's' daughter, in the garden watch her play
Out collecting herbs and mushrooms, roots and bark with growing moss
Feeling things an' climbing trees, always gaining, never loss

No single path is quite the same; that's not the nature of the game
The game is one, in each unique, be not afraid to take a peek
Expanding out in all directions, everything you see is found
All is then within your reach, just listen, hear the power in *sound*

Every bean a seeker be, if that's the truth you want to see!
To simply say 'i can', 'i do', will co-create the truth for you
'Tis simply fear that holds you back, don't live awareness in a lie
The truth is you can have it now, to see the light before you die

And so, these beans so young and pure of thought and word and deed
Have nurtured growth through dedication, with a love towards the seed
Each will walk a path that brings awareness new then every day
Everything with god is good and all the world can be ok

Observe the choices made and see, the same can be a truth for thee
Decisions then, the choice, the game, for all of us it's just the same
I'll see you there; same destination, all upon the learning curve
Same source an' path, same thoughts engaging, all emotion just the same

Sophie felt a deep contentment in the presence of the bean
Patience, love and tolerance, was in the other always seen
Honest words of love unfettered, simply all the couple knew
Physical was years away, grow in love that's pure and true

Undemanding love is true, it lays no rules and regs on you
Unconditional, divine, it's all the same, relax it's fine
Step by step in space and time, no slice is wrong in time and space
Just let your heart grow as it will and live your life, there's no disgrace

~*~

19

Glandwey goblin pushed her dogs to smell and seek and kill
Each contest was a pleasure, as she sought to find and keep the thrill
Racing, fire 'n' brimstone pulsing deep within their bulging veins
Never had they seen such strength, the seven dogs with all their chains

The dogs, a special goblin breed, were crossed with death and evil's seed
Great teeth to rip and tear and crunch, this really was a scary bunch
Their names were pride and greed and lust, and know them all i feel you must
So, gluttony and envy come to mind as well as wrath,
The final beast to cheat us all, you know that would be sloth

Yet swift these evil demons are, to rob you of your earthly life
To build and build upon emotion, causing trouble, causing strife
So, have a mind to be their master, not to share their worldly ways
Careful when you think of pleasure, mind your heart, protect your days

Through darkened wood, o'er frozen stream,
where e'er they hunt, the nose is keen
And for this task, their hearts are set, this is for pleasure, not for bet
To win the prize, to rip the flesh, to crunch the bone of all the nesh
To rest then when the task is done, so long since we have seen such fun

That afternoon they drank and ate, and planned an' plotted not so much
In fact, some drank excessively, and now to walk would need a crutch
As evening came and darkness fell, klaus sent them out to search for bell

And as he watched the team depart, then scurried back to loft above
A love for self, grew deep inside, saw not, the shadow of the dove
Not so much the love from others, in the mirror, eyes are fixed
Just himself beneath the covers, never, are there fluids mixed

Glandwey goblin stopped outside the village walls to get the smell
Communicating thoughts of death, was strawberry angel nearing hell?
Her dogs began to strain and spit, saliva sloshing through theirs gums
The growls of camaraderie, a hunting party full of chums!

The truth of course with killers, meanies, evil thoughts of every kind
All self-serving, false, deceivers, hard it is a friend to find
All can change though, truth to see, with love to nurture, set you free
I can't tell you or cajole, it's up to you to save your soul

A sniff, and they were on their way to find the strawberry angel dear
More confusion still to come? we see it daily, (true), i fear
The clack and spit of acorns spinning underfoot of goblin seen
Will she find the bell or compass, will she build von stroodle's dream?

The crooning crows had flown the pub, no rush was true, least as they thought
With wings to cover ground so quick, it's time for food, as time was bought
So off to road and field and tree, to scan with eyes for food to see
Though only three were here today, the rest it seems gone off to play

Boris, bill and bob were tight, together every day and night
Were part of a much bigger crew that numbered all of twenty-two
A crew within a crew they found, secured their days upon the ground
Relying, well, on just a few, is such an easier thing to do

And as they flew and hopped and walked, then of this task each one then
talked
The outcome, while it seems so grand (well only if all goes as planned)
Just serves a single, just the one, not really sharing, not much fun
So boris, bill an' bob decide to seek more answers 'bout this stuff
Besides, old klaus is often nasty, such a bully, always gruff

With a certain equanimity, avoiding then the apathy
The crooning crows, as such they were, decided they would ask the bean
"We'll find him, then we'll simply ask him who he is, what's going on?
And when he tells us what we want, we'll thank him with a crooning song"

And so, they all continued on, a plan they had agreed in mind
To get the answers from the bean and so this bean they had to find
He may be at the place he sleeps or even very far away
We all know how the beans will wander, finding new in every day

all forms of life, progress as seekers
seekers all, *towards the light*

~*~

20

Within the darkened forest, though the moon doth shine on high so bright
Smell no footsteps, see no sound; nonsense, look, is running free
In between the blades of moonlight, trees as shadows in the night
Mischief also on the ground, pairs up with nonsense, tough for thee

The little house with chimney smoke, within a clearing there it stood
A pretty house with doors and windows, made of brick and glass and wood
Curtains hung at side of windows, knocker waited on the door
A stack of wood for fire was waiting, welcome mat upon the floor

The house belonged to 'enid wick', a witch for sure, though no one knew
Could do a trick if ever pushed, her glasses always seemed askew
Her jacket 'tweed', her skirt was too, brown leather brogue, that was her shoe
Her hair was always in a bun, with wispy tassels flowing down
A toffee always in her teeth, with toffee wrappers all around

She started eating in her car, to curb the need to smoke cigar
They get stuck to her teeth a lot, but dentures never really rot
An ancient hippy through and through, who seeks to walk the path divine
Her love is unconditional, her days are blurred but still sublime

"Without regard to time or space, but of the content do be sure"
The voice preceded enid wick, who waltzed out magically through door
"Ef, that you?" young strawberry whispered, eyes were full of enid wick
"Hear my voice and feel my fear, it's not the time to play a trick!"

"Strawberry angel, darling fairy, dearie i've been watching you
Ever since you got the compass, then decided what to do"
Enid walked a dainty step and paused between each two or three
Walked towards the strawberry angel, cocked her head to clearly see

"I don't know how you came by such an object, but it's not for you
It's meant for beans like me, to change the colour, find the perfect hue
Come my dear, let's go inside and i shall tell you all i know
Of how i seek illumination, seek my very soul to grow"

Enid wick was so excited, she must keep it deep inside
Turned to walk back in the cottage, legs began, increased in stride
Glanced behind to see if strawberry walked towards the door as well
Strawberry checked, saw nothing that suggested this could be a hell

Enid wasn't evil and she didn't mean to be unkind,
It seems she simply wants a 'thing', and so would kill for her to find
Strange no bean can ever see how 'coveting' they are
Money, polished stones and metal, lots of stuff, a house, a car

And even enid wick the witch, it seems could never see
The purpose of magnetic needle, here to help the beans go free
"The compass, it was give' to me by merddyn, there, i tell you true
There's a warning, better take it, else his wrath will fall on you"

"Merddyn? well, i never did, that name unspoken for so long
A nonsense sadly, strawberry angel, he'll not help you in this song
Years and years of buried hatreds, stolen loves and treasures lost
Fantasies and legends blur, merddyn melts as sun on frost"

Slowly then the angel walked, as though it seemed there was no choice
A magic spell upon the limbs? "arms and feet will hear my voice"
Enid smiled back at strawberry, who now knew, she read her mind
Well almost, sometimes, that was certain, is she evil, cruel, unkind?

Seems all things are just perspective, based upon your point of view
Enid might drink tea or coffee, strawberry drinks a special brew
Enid witch, she is a bean, strawberry angel is a fairy
Different ways in different worlds, breaching planes, dimensions new
Whatever will poor strawberry do, outcomes here could be quite scary...

Enid sent the fairy to the chair that sat by fire so bright
Soon it would be evening and the room would need to see a light
Enid smiled and went towards a cupboard by the big front door
She opened up its squeaky face, she took two candles, then two more

She placed them all about the room and lit them all without a match
Then went towards another door and opened it by lifting latch
She squeezed her lips and kissed the air, like calling, but no one was there
Until he slowly swaggered, swaying, curled himself around the door
He palmed his ear, oh, several times, then licked and licked to preen
The cat was coming in this room, a champion supreme

He owned the place, and that he knew, he flopped and rolled around the floor
As for the mouse that wasn't there, he laboured at it with his paw
He smelt the fairy, smelt the flesh, the fairy flesh must taste so sweet
He was a feline after all, so always sank his teeth in meat

"Boobie, boobie mummy's boy, have you come out to play?
Hungry? want some food or water? guess what mummy found today!"
Enid rubbed his furry belly, made him purr and curl his head
Seemed like he was sleeping, maybe? anywhere becomes a bed

"I'll get you fish for dinner, kitty, keep you whole and keep you full
Then rest and sleep in window sun, upon my scarf that's made of wool
Cos i know what yer thinking kitty, little bugger that you are
Smell the little strawberry angel, want to eat her, how bizarre"

Enid clicked her fingers and the cat became all stiff and still
Then in a flash was running and he jumped up onto window sill
Another click and there's a bowl, with fishes in it one, two, three
The cat gave in to magic and began to eat the freshest tea

Enid turned to strawberry angel, "where's my manners, dearie me
Perhaps you'd like a glass of water, something stronger, coffee, tea?"
Strawberry sat, was sort of stuck, but moved her eyes and head
She looked towards the cat sat eating, thought on all the witch had said

"Some water please, sounds quite refreshing, hope it's cool and fresh and
clear"
Enid clicked a silver thimble, "lovely, there you are my dear"
Enid warmed to strawberry angel, liking manners given free
Everything was going great, it's like she's just popped round for tea

Tricky little strawberry angel, only freed her arms she did
She needs her arms to drink the drink, she'd wait to launch her freedom bid
The water tasted as it should, she smiled at enid, took a drink
Then noticed enid look at cat and to the cat she gave a wink

The drink it wasn't poisoned, wasn't sending any one to sleep
The water really tasted good, the thimble she would try to keep
And now we see the reason, why she had to try to free her arm
To save herself with magic and remove herself from enid's charm

All fairies carry wands of course, and strawberry fairy had one too
A special, tiny little wand, she kept it safely in her shoe
That's why the witch had trapped her so, denied her using either arm
Deny the use of magic wand, remove the threat, remove the harm

Each was wary of the other, magic spells they could bring forth
Chanting by the 90 round, to east and west and south and north
But as is almost always found, the threat caused fear, seen uncontained
It's strange how beans dismiss their will, it's all to do with how they're
trained

'Do to them before they do the very thing to me'
Mean and spiteful, not that loving, neither will it set you free
Just simple thoughts are entertained, the fear just drives the evil high
Find a generous disposition, negativity deny

Strawberry drew her wand and flashed a bolt at enid, hit the wall
Enid dived for cover, smashing vase i wouldn't say was tall
Not that nimble, enid really, built for comfort, not for speed
Still, with all her witchy efforts and her skill she would succeed
At least that's what she liked to think and mostly found it true
Would strawberry get the upper hand, time to see a different view?

Sadly no, she hit the fairy with a blast of plasma fuzz
It pinned her up against the wall and shocked her body with the buzz
Enid hid behind a chair, but gathered up upon her knee
The blast was bright, the room was dusty, had to wait and then would see

If strawberry angel took a tumble, was the fight now over, done?
Would this be her final rumble? bit too quick and not much fun!
When strawberry took the hit and felt the buzz and dropped down onto floor
The cat just flipped his lid, ran up the curtain, on the back of door
Through dust and smoke she crawled to hide behind the sofa and the wall
Her little wand, in little hand, her dainty feet, were all so small

Her heart was big, her courage true, a fairy always took a stand
And strawberry wasn't ordinary, slightly different, tricks in hand
She stood and shook, removing dust, a cloud before her fell to floor
"You think you've had enough of me, well i'm about to give you more"

She said some words and waved her wand, then tapped herself upon the nose
And what was there to see was gone; no fairy, wand, no shoes, no clothes
She rushed out from the cover of the sofa and the wall
Of course, the witch did not respond, for she could see no thing at all

Strawberry waved her wand again and matter fizzed and popped an' cracked
And enid watched the spot where air and wand and matter hissed an' smacked
She traced the path and aimed to catch the angel with a mighty blow
The tip of wand got really hot as energy began to glow

She let it rip, it curved in air as though was tracking too,
Escape then, maybe pointless, seems there's not that much that you can do
Strawberry took the hit and... BANG!

The blow was just too much for her, she lay upon the floor
Not a movement came from her, the cat still clung to back of door
The dust clouds filled the room and slowly settled on the ground below
The carpet, arms of chair an' cushions, all seemed dusted white with snow

The cat jumped down from back of door and walked towards the angel fair
He saw her damaged frame there lifeless, all messed up her strawberry hair
He poked her with a paw and sniffed, he always liked a game or two
He saw her gentle sleeping face, her little wand, her little shoe

Enid came and pushed him gently, picked up strawberry with her hand
Placed her on a velvet cushion, things had not gone quite as planned
Sometimes the way things work, it seems, we'll never understand
The way you feel a pain, distortion, there's no link, no touching hand

Unbeknownst to all, a certain fairy followed on behind
A friend with whom she felt a bond of love as rare as you could find
Together since the day of birth, when both brand new and oh so small
Rarely would you hear a problem, falling out, or hear a squall

Witnessing the evil deed, the error made the fury high
Always there for friends in trouble, fight until the end or die
Found a way to be within, so fortunate, so small and thin
Saw her strawberry laid there, dying? daisy formed the power within

"What's that feeling, what's occurring, who would be in here with me?
Manifesting magic power, seeks revenge and grows in thee
Show yourself and stand before me, i'll not strike thee down too quick
Have a chance to test the power, test the power of fairy tricks"

As she spoke she slowly crept, to twist and turn this way and that
She looked at window, looked at doorway, looked and winked at big black cat
The cat began to walk, then jumped up high upon the window sill
A prime position now adopted, strawberry angel he could kill

There she lay upon the cushion, motionless and still not breathing
Daisy watched the pantomime, the cat, the fear, her chest was heaving
Her wand held tight within her hand, the plasma power might explode?
the cat, to goad, he leapt at strawberry; daisy let him have the load

The full force caught the body square, the cat was smashed upon the wall
Twas then that enid witch, she screeched and howled and sought to break his
fall
But lust for anger and revenge would fire emotion, blind and strong
Inherent power, carnal nature, kill most any one, this song

A darkness then descended like no other had before it come
And were this not a tale of wonder you might ask 'what of the sun?'
The darkness there reflects the hate and evil lurking in our minds
'Tis sad there seems so much around, a poor excuse, a *sign of times*

Enid cornered daisy fairy, not a word could enid say
Anger had cut off her senses, same with every game we play
Daisy frozen on the spot, the plasma flow it crept to heart
Controlled and evil, like a torture, inch by inch a piercing dart

It touched the flesh of daisy fairy, shocked and overcharged her brain
Fade to black, no more sensation, would she ever be the same?
"Tried to save your friend my pretty, such a noble thing to do
Not so nice you hurt my kitty, such a pleasure killing you"

~*~

Merddyn's eyes sprung open, just as space/time turned to time and space
A single slice you can peruse, to see things *still* before your face
Forwards, backwards viewing time, to glean an understanding true
"Strawberry, daisy? danger, death? perhaps there's nothing i can do!"

It's hard for all to see the fate as chosen by yourself, you know?
To grasp and understand that fate's for learning lessons; off you go
If we just knew the truth in living, what's the nature of our game
Death would be a celebration, task fulfilled, you're not the same!

~*~

21

Al the bean was stuck on task, by choice, and wasn't in a rut
He sat in quiet meditation; from the tree? a "tut tut tut"
The crows, that's boris, bill and bob, had called to catch the eye of bean
But being deep in meditation, not a bird was heard or seen

And so, they all jumped down to lawn and hopped with caution t'ward the house
With little chirps and flaps of wing, they weren't as quiet as a mouse
Yet al the bean, he didn't move, as though were stuck in dream or groove
Suddenly one got distracted, seemed to then affect the mood,
Suddenly staccato marching, look around, there's tons of food

The bean of course though never far, with tethered cord was quite a way
Exploring aspects of the hue, correct within, that's how we play
Balancing the green, the substance from the touch, and balance mind
Adjust the thoughts, reactions, seek detachment, and the wise to find

The crows, while digging down for food and walking round the garden lawn
Almost forgot why they were there, they're not so much the devil's spawn
'til one of them bumped into al and tried dig into his shoe
It's made of skin called leather, so it's not an easy thing to do

He gave a peck, a stab or two, then cocked his head to see the leg
He turned and walked away a bit, then spun as though on single peg
He squawked and crowed, his mates joined in, it really was an awful din

With focus back, they climbed his leg and perched upon his knee
One would knock the other off, as each would try the bean to see
Boris sat alone and looked on all the fuss and noise next door
Bill and bob could be so silly, knocking each upon the floor

"Oi", said boris, "what's the game? you know what we are here to do
Bill, just sit upon his arm, and bob, stop trying to dig the shoe"
While each felt sort of castigated, smiles were never far away
There wasn't much in life that fazed 'em, even fear was part of play

The three were in position, a concerted effort they would make
They'd jump upon the limbs of bean, until the bean was wide awake
Up and down, the crows, they jumped, and not a squawk did any make
Instead they dug their talons in, so long and thin like fang of snake

Back into the garden came the body of the bean
His body's golden particles were sparkling yet were rarely seen
Bob fell off the body's knee and nearly fell to ground
Whilst flying up bob turned a bit an' squawked at what he'd found

The crows could see his astral form, though never had they seen one so
With more surprises yet to come... if you're the one that's in the know
For all the crows jumped off real quick, they flapped and squawked, afraid
they were
The panic maximised the fear, how long 'til they could all concur?

Seconds passed as calm returned, they turned and all surveyed the bean
Then cast their eyes back t'ward the sparkle, wonder like they'd never seen
The bean (the sparkle), spoke to them, which caused in them a start
Curiosity was stronger, soon their fear it did depart

"Who are you?", said bob unknowing, "why d'you sparkle like the sun?
Where d'you come from, where you going, why d'you spoil all our fun?"
They fired questions at the bean, the *sparkly* one that's rarely seen
Who calmly sat upon the grass and waited for the fear to pass

"It's so, so nice to see you all, and stop to have a chat
I wonder if you'd be so friendly if you thought I was a cat!"
The bean, he chuckled, felt amused, the crows stood staring, just bemused
"A cat, you know, it chases you, it tries to eat you too"
"D'you always talk like this?" said bob, "what about a 'how d'you do?'"
The (sparkly) bean, began to nod, not known for being an awkward sod

He understood the crows' dilemma, and so began to speak again
The manners, such a lovely fella, wouldn't want to be a pain
He said "i'm just a form of him", pointing to the other... sim?
I walk this way in meditation, done with purpose, not with whim

Boris strutted up to al and hopped upon his knee to speak
"Are you the one that spoke to badger, bertimus, the gossip freak?"
Before the words were out his mouth, his feet and claws fell through his leg
'Well this is weird', ol' boris thought, perhaps for mercy they should beg

"A wizard? no, it's as I said, I meditate out of my head
I like to go and do stuff while I can; i've got the chance,
You never know what's coming next, while engaged inside the dance"

The bean got up and walked towards the wooden fence so near his height
He pictured crows upon the same, expected it with all his might
And just as summoned, so it was, the crows towards the fence they sped
The talking, it was easy now, the crows were level with his head

" I didn't mean to spoil your fun, though using me, that's just not nice
You kept on digging claws in me, not once or twice but thrice
And then of course it begs the question, were you trying to wake me up?
I would say of course you were, seeing as you were jumping up!"

"And so, I came to help you, did you want to talk to me
For I can understand your words, but not like that, you see?"
Boris nodded, all concurred, three heads they seemed as one
Up and down the beaks would roll, observing sparkly bean in sun

"Ok", said boris, "here's a question, why does stroodle spy on you?"
He turned his head to wink at others, thought he'd tricked him, thought he knew
"Interesting", bean replied, "the badger also spoke that name
Are you aware of what i'm doing, of the nature of my game?"

"Well no, the pig, (that's stroodle), sent us, just to spy, to spy on you
But we're just nosey, ain't we fellas, what's all this about a hue?"
"Ah, the colours", said the bean, " the energies and auras too
Are just the sort of thing you need if you would be a brighter you"

"Every bean possesses power, power they can harness here
Never is the option lost, even though the change draws near
Nothing out, can serve their needs, only that that's found inside
But none will ever seem as me, unless they quell their fear and pride"

"I seek to balance, every day, in what I think and what I say
Compassion found, for all I have, and love, I found it too
Your every wish is your desire, just co-create for you
Express, expand and never judge, forgiveness eases life
'Understand' about the balance, not all things are seen as strife"

"Sadly, beans refuse to see the error of their chosen ways
And so, continue living in a deep confusion all their days
They trick themselves, ('well that's enough, i've done my bit to see')
Will they see god, i've no idea? who knows what's on the cards for thee"

Al began to walk away, "i need to rest while on my fast
It's all about preserving 'it', it's how we get the oil to last"
He slowly walked and turned and sat within the form so still and warm
And after moments, drew a breath, he shuddered once, it was the norm

Then once again the birds came up and jumped upon a solid limb
Boris looked at al and said "a sqwarkaluc-alakkowhimb"
"Ah", said al the *solid* bean, the crow then cocked his head
"Communication's down old bean, it seems the line is dead"

Al got up, the crows flew off and landed in a tree
Boris wondered of the bean, how only time will tell
If he would seek to steal the compass and the scared fairy bell
Will it all just simply end with... what's the benefit for me?

~*~

22

Gladys had a lovely house, with bedrooms six, for all to share
She'd lived there over 30 years, for moving on she had no care
The mums, they had a room for each, the children had one too
A bed, a wardrobe, chest of drawers, a window with a view

Sophie had a lovely room of cooling blue and warming white
She always felt so safe, secure, it seems the balance was just right
She often sat there during day while dreaming of a different hue
Seems almost every moment spent is contemplating being new

This bean was also on a fast, to speed and keep the process pure
This journey is the oldest one, no secrets here, it's not obscure
Diving in the silence deep to learn of balance as she should
See every learning curve with favour, every tree as part of wood

Sophie liked to nana-nap, not every day of course,
Recharging up her batteries, resolve to reinforce
It really was a little nap, of thirty mins or so
She laid her head upon her bed, there's nowhere else to go

That afternoon she fell asleep so quickly and so deep
Another world of inner dreams with secrets there to keep
And so, towards lucidity, to now enjoy a game
A boundless world of love and laughter; evil creeps, secures a chain

So many forms of life and light to always help you through
Whatever plays upon your mind is linked to dreams and comes to you
Connections varied, so unsure, the reasons for? they never change
The love, it just connects us all, there's nothing here to rearrange

Sophie, well, she was aware of black and darkness near and far
But lucid dreaming's fun; create a door and see it there ajar
Enough; the dark, the doom, the gloom, go through the door, another room
create and find a sea of green and fill with every kind of bloom

She wandered through the sea of love, the birds, the bees, the songs, the buzz
And next she came upon a stream, the first was here, a little fuzz
She saw it in the water, pops 'n' crackles, then a little splash
As quickly as it came it went, she felt no need to quickly dash

She stood upon a boulder in the middle of the stream
Dark clouds overhead they came and quickly changed the dream
The sun was gone, it caught her eye, she searched for light up in the sky
Upon the bank was roy the rat, and by his side, a big black cat

The water round the boulder started moving, spinning, faster round
She felt uneasy, "this is lucid", started co-creating ground
The boulder started wobbling, her balance it was gone
The cat stood up as though to leap, she wondered what was going on

"Remember this is just a dream", the rat said as the wind it came
The growing roar of rolling thunder, this is now a different game
Twas then the lightning struck the boulder, splitting it in two
Sophie started falling, it was then the water grew

It grew and grew, and formed a spiral chased and pushed by swirling winds
If only she could find control an' trace the thought, and that exscind
'BANG'...a blast of plasma fizz came through the swirling water wall
It caught her on the shoulder, she was flying so she couldn't fall

She felt the pain, the burning, as the plasma seared and burnt her flesh
Retaliation growing, she's a fighter, never seen as nesh
The cat, it howled and leapt from bank, she heard the screeching, heard the wail
The cat had launched a full attack, with ripping claws and whipping tail

She somersaulted tumbling, the cat she wrestled under arm
For all the love she felt inside, it seems she was about to harm
She grabbed the legs and arms of cat; her plan was soon to let him go
A shame that she forgot his teeth, so as for plan, well that's a no

Excruciating was the pain, the crimson hue of flowing blood
Twas then a spark came into mind an' "STOP", and so there was a thud
Fighting off the foe, the cat, the rolling, thrashing on the bed
All dimensions are connected, fell on floor and bumped her head

"Ow", she groaned, and gently rubbed her aching brow and stood
She walked towards the window and looked out towards the wood
Her eyes traced back to garden wall, and who d'you think she saw
A grinning rat and vanquished cat, all tied and gagged upon the floor

She blinked and double blinked again, she rubbed her eyes and they were gone
Tried to find a clue, a meaning, see how everything went wrong
She thought of all the things that happened, walked the sequence of events
Perhaps it's just the way of dreams, rarely making any sense

Al the bean came into view... she smiled

~*~

23

Freddy falcon seemed to almost float above the silbury hill
Calm, relaxed, his belly full, there was no need to spot a kill
Instead he simply soared on high, the upward draughts his wings to bear
He turned and rolled and twisted, doing acrobatics in the air

While talons, beak and wings are deadly, things you need to make the kill
Freddy's body had another, had another special skill
Eyes to see a thousand yards to spot a tiny mouse or shrew
Speed and other deadly weapons, nothing more that you could do

As he circled, swooped and dived, a flash of light just caught his eye
He banked his wing to change his course, to *use* the wind, would rarely force
Another flash, to focus in, then heard a 'BANG', a mighty din,
'BANG' another, from a clearing, down on darkened forest floor
"No rush, no rush, just take your time, above in circles I could soar"

"Never one to rush in where some others fear to tread
Unless of course, you spot a kill; you just dive in and then they're dead
Adjusting angles on the wing, the wind streams over beak and face
Survey it all and search for clues, gliding down at gentle pace"

"Well, is that who I think it is?" the falcon was surprised
Friend or foe they're all the same, someone's just been recognised
He veered a little off his course, a meeting now was on the cards
Gliding gently down to landing, sixty, forty, twenty yards

A branch selected for his weight, his talons locked to hold him still
The counter balanced tail 'n' head, he bobbed and weaved to look until
He saw her cruising on her skates of acorns, drawn by seven dogs
She swerved to miss the trees, the bushes, fallen branches, ancient logs

Glandwey goblin cracked her whip up in the air above her boys
No need to tingle flesh of dog with all possessions classed as toys
The noise of progress grew until the falcon perched above her head
He called her with a screeching cry so sharp would even cut the dead

She turned and saw the falcon watching, now behind her, couldn't see
"AHH", she grunted to the bird, and saw a gap past coming tree
The left-hand rein, she yanked it back and gently leaned in to the curve
Her face was grinning ear to ear, such 'joie de vivre' and steely nerve

She arced a perfect arc and gently slowed to stop below the bird
The setting sun annoyed her eye, to ease the strain, his wing unfurled
"What d'yer think of that then 'falcky', cheeky grin and playful grunt!"
Even though relieved she was, for compliments she seemed to hunt

Though really it was just a tease, to pass the time and have some fun
She changed position, moved a bit, to block the light from setting sun
"Good, yeah, really good", said freddy, "want to go again?
I'll race you round the circle twice, to have a laugh, a game"

No sooner had the final words slipped out his mouth, and she was off
She groaned and grunted cracked her whip, and freddy falcon (startled),
coughed
And straaained, he thrust torso forward, launched himself into the air
Pulled his wings with power, precision, a fighting spirit, not despair

Along the path she took before, she cracked the whip to speed the pace
She growled and shouted at the dogs, to egg them on, to win the race
Freddy's line of curvature was slightly longer, had to be
Power and speed are great, but you need space to fly around tree

The inside line for glandwey goblin, freddy took the outside ring
Inside shorter, outside slower? who would hear a winner sing?
Glandwey did the ninety, past a hundred, leading by degree
But freddy's power and speed and skill just seemed to edge in front of she

Glandwey's eyes, they turned to slits,
she growled and cracked her whip once more
Her feet grew warm, the acorns steamed,
from spinning 'cross the forest floor
The dogs found strength from where was none
and all screamed past the setting sun
There's malice in the minds of players; always starts as simple fun

She cracked her whip, caught feather tip, the falcon scowled and dipped his wing
With twist and turn he flew past tree, a lead for freddy soon to see
"The cheat, the scoundrel", freddy thought, "a lesson glandwey must be taught"
She edged in front, a hoot with glee, bit premature? we'll shortly see

Freddy took a wide bank right, then sharply cut back 'cross the line
Shot past the face of glandwey goblin, nicked her cheek, a cut so fine
The rage of competition coursed its way through pumping vein
The blood, the pain came quickly on, a small distraction just the same

With eyes off path, she didn't see the massive boulder up ahead
The dogs, they swerved, upended glandwey, rolled and kissed a tree with
head
The speed, the power, the thrust, the crash, the need has gone for her to dash
The falcon circled round once more, then found a branch to sit and see
The dogs with all their tails wagging, licking blood from face and tree

The glandwey goblin soon recovered, pushed the crazy dogs away
Then looked up into tree at freddy, looking down upon the fray
"You cheated and you cut me", said the goblin full of piss 'n' vim
"That ain't no way to run a race, it ain't no way to win"
The goblin just dismissed her wounds then stood and jumped to grab the bird
"To think that you could capture me? the thought is really too absurd"

Out of reach he sat there looking, salivating at the 'red'
"You cheated first, you whipped my wing,
And that's why you just bumped your head"

" Cheat", she hissed towards the ground and huffed just once, to show disdain
She checked herself, her skates, her armour, never would she talk of pain
"I thought you should be at the top, not down here racing trees with me"
"I was", said freddy, "flying high; but something caught my eye, you see"

He used his wing to point the way and nodded just to do the same
As if was there for all to see, she squinted, tried to hold the frame
"There's a clearing up ahead, saw two flashes, then *bang bang*!
Diverted when I saw you coming, pulled along by canine gang"

"Thinking of the strawberry angel, haven't seen her come this way
And as you're here you haven't either, something's gone awry I say
Move towards the cottage yonder, i'll go back an' speak to klaus
Understand there may be danger, move as quiet as a mouse"

A flash of wings and freddy's off and steering round both bush and tree
Then zooming up to race along the top of forest canopy
The height advantage, so forgiving, errors ever rarely found
Circle once and then again, until your destination's found

~*~

24

M erddyn sat in deep of hollow, in the cavern underground
Contemplating of the fellow, of the bean, the lover found
Free of chains of space/time, wander fully through the past
Scan the time/space slices, observations, have a net to cast

All is there tomorrow, the beginning and the end
All is lessons learned in love, forever curving round a bend
Merddyn searched awareness as a playground for the love he held
Letters forming words, and yet it's bliss that all is ever spelled

The balance throws the feeling off, the ripple through a heart and mind
Project we can, our thoughts of error, so unloving, so unkind
Truth is in awareness, in awareness where a merddyn sat
Of error laden thoughts and deeds, projected by a witch and cat

Within an instant mark the change, the earthly coat donned once again
He stood, the seven senses keen to help negotiate terrain
To shift to owl and flap thy wing, no sound or whisper, voice to sing
Through cloak of darkness could he fly, then undetected in the sky

He soared his way through darkened forest, left and right past sleeping tree
Saw his way to find a clearing, strawberry - daisy there to see
He landed on a branch of tree that stood a spit from cottage door
So spat some bones of mouse from gut, that knocked on wood, then fell to
floor

'Tat-tat-tat-tat', the knock it sounded, "who the dickens could that be?"
Said enid witch, caught unawares, intent to go outside and see
Merddyn hopped a little up, away and out of sight of eye
So each advantage must we grasp, to find the breeze that helps us fly

The door swung open, enid crossed the threshold looking out for clues
Sought assistance from a helper, summoned broom with click of shoes
"Precious, look around for me, for anything or anyone
That seems... well sort of out of place, then let me know, i'll get the gun"

The broom then seemed to wag a tail it clearly didn't have
Moved off quite slowly, ever speeding, sort of like the speed of grav'
The end of handle bent a bit as though it had a nose
Then flew about as ordered, sniffing, searching for? well, no one knows

Within a second, maybe more, the broom was back, it banged on door
Enid answered "that was quick, go back to where you were before"
Enid's head did twitch a bit, from left to right and up and down
Slowly banking, then was twisting, always moving t'ward the ground
Then up and to the left did see, the big old owl hid up the tree

So slowly did she walk towards the middle of her little yard
Her wand slid down her sleeve to grip between the fingers, poised to strike
The energiser, set in gold upon her finger, sits the sard
Glowing more and drawing power, nature's power, up to spike

Merddyn formed, in all with gown, and gently floated down to ground
Within a golden sphere of light, the timeless walker drew her sight
And enid witch, in awe she froze, from top of head to tip of toes
But not from any spell be sure, except a mind that's weak, unsure

A momentary suck of breath, an image forming from the past
Of ancient, old and wonders true, of things they said could never last
"You be merddyn, be it true, you say it's not, I challenge you"
She whipped her wand out, spun it round, and hopped about upon the ground

"Oh, very good, I love a dance, tai chi magic, 'horsey prance'?
Nice to see some variations of the tried and trusted ways
Seems perhaps a million years, with each an infinite of ways
Don't really see that much that more, no hands, no wands, it's all top drawer"
He tapped his head then tapped his heart, and from her sight he did depart

Inside the cottage merddyn stood, he looked about and froze the cat
Then waited for an enid to come calling, knocking, 'tat-tat-tat'
The door burst open, in she flew, banged into wall and dropped a shoe
She gathered focus up to see a sea of plasma energy

A stream of never-ending plasma flowed from tip of magic wand
Crackling, screeching, fizzing, pinging, mystifying any sonde
And merddyn simply swallowed it, and too, began the gargle song
Enid looked and listened baffled, conjured up a plasma bomb

Merddyn didn't move or wink or raise an arm to strike a blow
Just simply thought and it was done, and enid looked but didn't know
Not where she was or how she got there, all she knew, she knew no more
Merddyn rested in the armchair, sent the cat and shut the door

The cat and enid stood and stared transfixed in time and space, a slice
To sit and think a while they can, they have the time, it would be nice
And as for strawberry and for daisy, there without a breath they lay
But a secret known by merddyn, he will share with us this day

Fairies and some others are eternals so they never die
Should the life force energy become expelled they sleep and lie
Waiting for another with a heart that's full of love and light
A love that's unconditional, to make the change and put things right

The fairies both receive from merddyn, truth to send them on their way
He will stay for more adventure, there's some games he wants to play
Artful teaser, sows the seeds of light and fun, deception true
Always keeping merddyn close, concerns, were he a foe to you

The fairies flew off side by side, and hand in hand towards the hill
The journey, always full of danger, other beasts the two would kill
The compass back where it should be, the quest returns to tease and goad
As merddyn sits and waits to see, who journeys there on *frog and toad*

~*~

25

It could have been just minutes passed, but freddy did so love to fly
To feel the wind upon the face, to search through cloud that hung in sky
To scour the ground that scurries by, to focus in on prey with eye
And soon enough he'd had his fun, for now at least, this round of sun

For soon the moon would be in sky, and all find light is not the same
Reflecting only bits of light, that's why the beans depend on flame
Soon enough the glide, the landing, outside where some tables are
Drinkers sat an' supped a brew, transfixed above by brightest star

Freddy flew through open window, skipped upstairs to stroodle's door
Banged his head against the woodwork, scraped his talons on the floor
"Enter", called a gruff pretender, silence waited for the move
Freddy jumped to grab the handle, flapped to open up the door

Once inside he told von stroodle all the things he'd seen and done
The observations, hours of hovering, bored just waiting, not much fun
Then things changed, the first explosion, then another, then BANG BANG
Von stroodle jumped up on his desk, he paced about then looked at gang

His mouth, it moved, he didn't shout, just forming words, but none came out
He looked to ceiling, looked to floor, then looked at freddy, looked at door
Freddy looked at molly mouse, she shrugged and sort of shook her head
Freddy thought of cosy trees and solid branches for his bed

"Freddy, you're the fastest flyer, quickest news delivery
With molly on yer back to guide you, in the darkness now you'll see
The boys have fashioned seat and harness, snug, to fit upon yer back"
Freddy gasped "am I nocturnal? seems yer mind's becoming slack"

Freddy didn't like it, no, he didn't like it, that's for sure
But klaus had promised double pay, so freddy prepped to fly through door
The harness fit him like a glove, did not restrict in any way
"The harness, just to keep her stable? all directions, simply say?"

"This isn't ruddy pilot school, you can't switch auto-pilot off
You're a bird an' she's a mouse, so stop yer chat and bugger off"

Molly smiled at freddy, climbed aboard, then they were on their way
Out the window, through the air; a perfect end to perfect day?
Not so much in freddy's mind, he has a point, one has to say
Perhaps he could adapt the plan, left or right, a little sway

~*~

Klaus von stroodle paced about his desk then stopped when they were gone
He didn't like the feel of things, this wasn't how he sang his song
"Just follow strawberry, get the compass, get the bell and then it's done
Except for bean on solsbury hill; are the two then linked as one?"

"Clues, the clues, they change,
then they stop telling you the things they know
The fogs of time and mystery begin to form and thicken so
So many hands would seek to hold the truths of time the beans have lost
I'll not meet failure this time round, i'll have my way at any cost"

Von stroodle banged his little fist into his other tiny hand
'Tis strange to think this guinea pig was feared the most in all the land
But such is power in words you speak, so you should have a care
To understand what drives all fear and be *your* master, be aware

100

For when you know the truth in purpose, know the secret of your life
  Most everything you do is fun and rarely visit pain or strife
  Lessons always in awareness, always draw the same to you
  Want to find a new beginning? simply pause and say "i do"

~*~

26

The seven dogs of glandwey goblin always pulled her every day
Forwards, backwards, left and right; not always *right*, I have to say
She was impulsive, quite aggressive, rarely paused for thought it seems
In and out of all awareness, change dimension, entered dreams

After freddy falcon flew to get instructions from the pig
She rested for a moment, sang a song and did a jig
She donned her skates of acorns and her armour made of acorn shell
The roller skates just made her happy, not that anyone could tell

So off towards the cottage in the clearing at a stealthy pace
The falcon said there could be danger, now we stroll, no need to race
As more and more seen through the wood, the cottage, it came into view
A certain '*je ne sais quoi*' feeling, "wonder what would freddy do?"

She paused unsure in hesitation, "just what could the danger be?
Maybe it's just strawberry in there, by the fire, having tea"
She left her dogs behind a bush and crept a little, paused in fear
Without the noisy dogs it seems, there's so much more that she could hear

Step by step she ventured forward, forward then, towards the door
Would this be her final journey, would she feel a monster's claw
'Click', a latch released, un-keeping, door from staying closed, shut tight
Opened then, a little creaking, time and age is heard this night

A witchy witch came into view, "I'm enid witch, how do you do?"
They shook their hands, "such clammy skin, and such a beauty too
Such matted hair, with bugs and more, what brings you calling at my door?"
Glandwey goblin seemed confused; "you're not a monster, got no claw?"

In vacant air, unfinished thoughts and words, will simply disappear
Perhaps the enid witch can help, restoring glandwey's faith in fear
"A monster, no, no, no, not me, perhaps an old and evil witch
Who sucks the flesh off bones of goblins, throws the rubbish in the ditch"

"You're welcome now to come inside, and maybe sit a while with me
Perhaps i'll have a look around and find some food to have for tea"
Glandwey goblin, while she wasn't always tops in smarts 'n' stuff
She had the sense to see when things were getting... well, a bit too rough

Slowly then she backed away, a bigger distance, more secure
Enid witch just stood there smiling, endless patience will endure
"I'm just looking for a friend that might have come your way
Sorry to disturb your evening, might come back another day"

Just before she turned to go, the witch gave out cackled laugh
"Come inside and dine with me, we'll work upon your epitaph"
Again she cackled, screeched and howled, her jokes it seemed she loved the most
"Come, let's get a feast on fire, can you guess the meat to roast?"

Off she flew into the air and swirled about poor glandwey's head
"Feel the darkness creeping on you, hear the voices of the dead?"
A wind blew up, the dogs they howled, like everybody knew
The ending of a goblin's life? a balancing of karma too?

The noise, the screams, the cries of death, the lightning flashes snapping trees
The storm it seems was overhead and caused in glandwey trembling knees
Full of fear and full of dread, the glandwey goblin tripped 'n' fell
Enid's face could get no closer, "feeling hot, like nearing hell?"

Again, a piercing, screeching cackle, enid flew then crashed to ground
Enid eyed the goblin shaking; "...more to say, so gather round"
Glandwey goblin rose upon her toes, transfixed by enid's stare
Her body dragged along the dirt, "listen well and have a care"

" I know why you've come here goblin, I know what you'd like to do
Strawberry angel, daisy fairy, tasty morsels both to chew
"I will eat the strawberry angel, I will keep the compass true
You will go and tell your master there was nothing you could do"

A flash of white, a cloud of smoke, the goblin sought no more the joke
The fear had set, and set real good, there's only danger in this wood
Glandwey mounted skates and pulled the dogs to turn around, go back
The way she came, that's back to village, use the dogs to find the track

Faster than she'd been before, she drove the dogs in dark of night
Never had she felt this way, never had she known such fright
Merddyn looked around the cottage, feeling here the job was done
He was here, then in an instant, disappeared like setting sun

~*~

27

If you've never flown before, well then, you will understand
The howling, wailing, crying of a mouse not on the ground
Well really, when you think about it, not so much surprise
Her head, it's full of images, "this can't be true, it must be lies"

Molly mouse had never seen the world from up above
Flying fast on freddy's back, to see as though were dove
"Things all shrinking down to nothing, even popping out of sight
It's not 'nat'ral', it's not right, it's evil what i've seen tonight"

Every now and then, when molly's howling got too much to bear
Freddy took a dive straight down, it caused a whistle in her hair
Her scream was just a constant, like a roller coaster ride
So freddy did a loop-de-loop, "she'll catch her breath, become tongue tied"

But no such luck for freddy, golly, molly was an awful nag
"Is there no way to shut her up, this constant whinging, whining hag?"
Deliverance it seems had come, a clearing up ahead
"SILENCE, there's the clearing, woman, hold your tongue or else be dead"

Freddy edged a tiny smile, a curling up on beaky lip
("A threat of danger shuts her up, we'll use that on the homeward trip")
But there, before they reached the clearing, what d'you that they could see
A team of dogs and glandwey goblin, skating fast between the trees

Molly mouse just pointed down, banking left and turning round
"I see her", said the falcon, and they glided down to meet the ground

Glandwey saw the landing party, saw them land just up ahead
Yanked the reins to slow her dogs, it seems she had control of head
And once the dust of dog team settled, wiping dust from mouth and eyes
Glandwey grinned, so rare and special, "isn't this a nice surprise!"

"You've brought a snack, is this a picnic; love me? maybe we could share?"
"You're not where you're s'posed to be, so hold yer tongue and have care"
Molly mouse was feisty, tough, upon the ground she had no fear
A light of some awareness new, freddy saw the balance here

Glandwey chuckled just a bit, still rolling from her quip before
As molly jumped from freddy's back and ventured down to forest floor
"Shouldn't you be at the house?" asked freddy still up in the tree
"I was", said glandwey goblin, "but a witch came out and threatened me"

The other two let out a gasp, "a witch", said molly with a crunch
Molly then, a little 'peckish', found a bug on floor to munch
"Said that she would eat the fairies, keep the compass, maybe more
'Tell yer masters that i've got 'em', went inside an' slammed the door"

Freddy looked at molly, back at glandwey, back at molly
"This is silly, there's no mention of a witch to block our way"
Glandwey shrugged her shoulders looking up at freddy in the tree
"I'm telling you that's how it was, it's not a lie, it's as I say"

Molly mouse ran up the tree, then sat again on freddy's back
"You go back to klaus an' tell 'im, we'll go on, i've had *my* snack"
"On to where, for what?" asked fred', "the compass now is surely gone"
"There's still the bell", said molly mouse, "all a part of single song"

Freddy launched himself, and her, towards the sky to fly once more
The moon was shining through a clearing, fluffy clouds of white, a door
Beams of light, they tickled ground, to light the way of all who find
Illuminations streaming in, to feed and grow the seeker's mind

And so to top of silbury hill, a tree was found to perch and see
As for the compass? who would know, if they should stay, if they should go
A key? a compass? which is which and what to who, a seed to sow?
An owl was heard to hoot, unseen, perhaps then there will be a show

Glandwey, left alone once more, began to move 'cross forest floor
Her dogs began to up the pace, strange, as now there was no race
Their muscles pumped and speed, it grew, was there a thing that she could
do?
Thoughts of the most evil kind began to seep into her mind

Such is fear, as fear you see, is one to play a trick on thee
In truth, there's none upon this land, could ever harm you with a hand
Thoughts are seeds within the mind, a place for them is yours to find
A thought that you've no wish to see, then simply discard from your tree

The strongest will of mighty men has fallen with the sight of pen
But understand as all should see, the *mind* is always *free* you see?
Onwards, ever onwards, always changing, it's the normal way
Will glandwey goblin reach the village, get to klaus and have her say?

~*~

28

After dinner, mums and gladys did the dishes, binned the scup
Two young beans on soulful journeys, lay in garden looking up
"I had a sort of nightmare while I slept this afternoon
A big black cat was trying to get me, stuck inside a wet typhoon"

"That's odd", said al, who closed his eyes and slowly seemed to drift away
"D'you get away, away to safety?" contemplating on his day
"I paused to look, to see, consider, crashed the whole with mental force"
"Ah, so you were lucid then!" "what? oh lucid, yes, of course!"

Al rolled over looked at sophie, tempted then to sit or kneel
"You ok, you seem distracted? things are going well, I feel
Can you feel the green beginning, feeding soul and then to heal?
The process doesn't seem protracted, we've no karma on the wheel"

"Yes, I know, it's all ok, I was just surprised I guess
Rolled off my bed and on the floor, banged my head and tore my dress"
"Wow", said al, "that's really busy, so much busier than me
I just sat and played some mind games with an owl asleep in tree"

"The dream gave me a certain feeling, here inside, was really strange
Do you think it had a bearing on a single thing we do?
Think of all the ways a situation seems to change
The different thoughts and choices, like they all are then brand new"

Al sat up and smiled at sophie, took her hand to press to cheek
"Soon we'll feel more light inside us, all in all, less than a week
Things then, just come back together, countless are the paths to choose
Let your thoughts just wander freely, there's no tricks, no cheats, no ruse"

Sophie smiled and closed her eyes, and al laid on the ground once more
Three old ladies smiling, waiting, peeking round a kitchen door
Lucky little beans, a chance was given to a favoured few
'Tis sad not many make the choice to dance and find a different hue

~*~

29

Strawberry angel, daisy fairy, each revived by love so true
Shared a special bond of love, so rare and found in very few
To know your love and always find within your heart the path of right
Will serve and feed you all your days; 'tis said from old that right is might

But understand the mighty mind, benevolence to all you know
Humility becomes a tool of love, to help your soul to grow
So many creatures, *all* created, learning all the time they are
Always see with kindly eyes and *draw your love from yonder star*

They hadn't spoken, not a word, since merddyn cast the love on each
But did inform each of the role the other took in battle done
In every moment of awareness, there are always things to teach
Things to think of, things to learn, done in anger, done in fun

Side by side they gently flew across the ground to rise up hill
Until the daisy fairy stopped, the thoughts in mind she had to spill
"Strawberry angel, know I loves yer, always will, I tell you straight
But words of jealousy and anger, from my mouth they slipped the gate"

"I told that klaus von stroodle of the journey you were going to make
The love for you that merddyn spoke of, leap of faith you had to take
It's my fault that the witch was waiting, my fault that she took your spark
Took away that new awareness, left your soul asleep and dark"

Daisy's tears began to swell and gently tracked across her cheek
So different now without the drink, so calm and gentle, mild and meek
"Daisy fairy, sister, wonder of my life and friend most dear
Embracing error's just a way to learn and rid ourselves of fear"

"Always will I love you, daisy, understand and care I do
Now you must forgive yourself, perhaps the hardest thing to do
But know you can and know you will, and i've a feeling you will see
How easily we manifest all kinds of things because we're free"

Daisy rushed into her arms, to give, and so receive, a love
That lifts the spirits, moves the mountains, all are gifts from up above
The unconditionally loving takes a yellow turning green
Sees compassion growing unabated, all becomes serene

Love grows green, a mighty hue, with love there's so much you can do
A source perhaps of all we know, the sun, the earth, and round we go
No need to filter love and light that shines upon us every day
Swallow whole, embrace the good, become the child, explore and play

Ever onward, so they ventured, on the quest to find a love
Daisy fairy, *all* forgiven, shadows in her heart, a dove
Strawberry angel holds the compass, safe and tight within her hand
Rolling over hills of green, goodbye yellow, golden sand

The moon, it stood and lit their way, love and light within its smile
Nurturing of mother nature, blending purpose all the while
Will they reach the top then, safely, will the fairy bell be found?
Who or what will be there waiting, friend of foe upon the ground?

~*~

30

Morris mole, unlikely spy, dressed head to toe in velvet black
Used his claws to dig the earth and push it hard behind his back
Over years of ditching dirt to make a network underground
Hollow tubes in all directions, sharing every little sound

Running freely on a road made smooth and round through straight and curve
Life in such a darkened place, the strongest bean it could unnerve
But for morris this was home, a road to run, with room to stand
Upon all fours, of course it's true, he knew it like the back of hand

A scurry here, a hurry there, to find his food and feel anew
The good vibrations ringing round, announcing every colour too
Each time he felt a sense of something, heard the sound and saw the light
Visions of the changing colour, in his mind so clear and bright

As with all, he felt and paused, to focus in upon the change
Unknowing then, and like us all, it's step by step, can't rearrange
A seed then sown within his heart, unknowing seekers all we be
For when the mole doth close his eyes, yes, even he descends the tree

Overcoming all with love that seemed to come from all around
Beyond the village, silbury hill, but solsbury hill, he's underground
"Could be stones and boulders maybe, solid, waves bounce off for sure
Denser, giving strong reflections", held his hand up, offered paw

"First there was the one and then the second, with an echo
Definitely not a third, the sound... ", he closed his eyes to sense
"The colour, yes the colour, all the differences in vibe and hue
That's what makes it seem so different, all the colours, they're brand new

Almost a eureka moment really, when you think of all
The things that one could think or miss, like which direction, floor or wall
He walked around a little bit and played it over in his head
Like all solutions found in life, he'd sleep upon it in his bed

Although he had a special place, just like us all, we call it home
Well morris was a restless sort and so was always prone to roam
His house was near the river, flowing gently through the gap in hills
Safely then, above the river, 'case it bursts it's bank and spills

But over years his tunnels and the network he had built, it grew
To run the lot would take perhaps the light of day or maybe two
And so he saw a need for little resting spots along the way
Somewhere he could rest or sleep, an hour, a night, to sit or lay

Every hundred lengths of mole, he dug a little resting space
He kept them bare, no sticks, no straw, no mirror to inspect his face
Slightly higher than the 'moleway', here's example twenty-two
A cosy little sleeping chamber, not a lot for one to do

The purpose then is simply rest as morris goes about his day
Of course, he mostly works at night, digging isn't work, it's play
Other beasties use the moleways, more than twenty-one to use
Stretching many thousand mole lengths, many routes for all to choose

Bugs that morris likes to crunch on, falling through the roof to floor
Running then, along the moleway, searching for an exit door
Often times as morris digs, a bug will come along and bump
Into the bum of morris diggin', such that it would make him jump

Spinning round he knows what's coming, maybe snack or maybe lunch
Grab the bug, from morris running, up until we hear a crunch
He really is a splendid fellow, faithful friend to one who seeks
Planning then the revolution, every step laid out for weeks

Poor old klaus the guinea pig, the one who wants to see it all
'Tis said that morris mole is blind, but never do we see him fall
Life for all is expectation, co-creating all we see
Effort based on 'sense' is nothing, like the flight of bumble bee

Beans believe they shouldn't fly, yet clearly, we can see they do
Such a silly carnal mind that seems to miss *all* near and true
Morris will still help his friend to realise all his worldly dreams
With plots as thick as richest honey, sweet success through deadly schemes

"So just a little nap then, for a half an hour, maybe more
Then once again i'll share the news, and scurry on the moleway floor
For now though, in this sphere of space, a room without a view is best"
He lay his head, he closed his eyes, and rested paws upon his chest

~*~

31

Late that night a quiet thunder, quiet thunder in the sky
Distant clouds sit still and menace, lightning flashes catch the eye
Rolling over hills the thunder, will the sky stay clear and true?
All is always as it should be, nothing then for you to do

Glandwey goblin rolled into the village with her dogs
The village had a quiet air, with all asleep like logs
Well, not completely all of them, for such were life and dreams
That klaus von stroodle paced his room, working on his schemes

Glandwey reached the village pub and saw the lights were burning bright
It seems more had a taste for night life, should've pulled the curtains tight
In she walked, her dogs around her, not unchained, but not confined
All the time the dogs would chatter, breed confusion in her mind

The someone at the bar was standing in for molly mouse
They poured a drink for glandwey goblin, "boss says this is on the house"
She took the drink and smiled, feeling special, very new
"This job ain't bad, it keeps me busy, no surprises, same old view"

"Boss upstairs?" asked glandwey goblin, "always, mostly", barman said
"How'd 'e know that I was coming?"; "klaus just gets things in his head
He shouted down before you got here, 'let her have a drink for free'
Them's the perks from our employer, 'what you get is what you see'"

Glandwey took her drink and dogs and slowly climbed the wooden stairs
Does klaus have some premonitions, couldn't catch him unawares?
Glandwey reached his office door and gently pushed it open wide
"Blimey, don't you know to knock"; "the door was open"; "come inside"

"And shut the door so no one enters, not without a proper knock"
"The door was open", she repeated, "alright, come on, you're on the clock"
"It's not good news", the goblin said, "no, not good news at all"
Klaus sucked in a massive breath, and held it in, on call

"Well?" he said expectantly, retaining of his breath
"Come on girl, i'm dying here, you're gonna cause me death"
Again, he sucked another breath, as glandwey stood to say
"A witch it was, she took the compass, said I should be on my way"

"'Go and tell yer boss', she said, 'i'll eat the strawberry fair
And i've the compass, mine to use, and i'm a witch, so best beware'"
"And was she?" klaus asked, getting angry, thoughts all racing round his head
"Plasma balls an' lightning flying, thought that I was surely dead"

Klaus leaned back, and looked at glandwey, sized her up as best he could
"So, plans to get it back then really wouldn't do us any good?"
He searched for hope, he clutched at straws, this was a blow, a blow for sure
Glandwey's head shook resolutely, "nothing more I could've done"
"Why'd it have to be like this, why'd she go an' spoil my fun?"

"I try so hard to sort this puzzle, every time it's just the same
Two steps forward, one step back, this is a most annoying game"
Glandwey edged towards the door and with a hand he shooed her out
"Stick around, i'll need yer later, have a drink, forget yer doubt"

She went downstairs and settled in while klaus was heard to shout and stamp
" All these ruddy fairy stories, dragons, castles, magic lamp
Witch, if you can hear me, come before me and i'll take you on"
Nothing happened, never did, 'tis sad he sang a blind man's song

~*~

32

Strawberry angel, daisy fairy, safe amidst a crop of stones
They can see the summit rise, a silhouette with trees as bones
On a distant line where love of earth meets distant sky
The faintest peaks of sun arising, so to arc before the eye

Each at rest, as needed, for a sleep as theirs can take its toll
Akin perhaps to losing life, if life were found inside a soul
To know inside, to be and see, through eyes of old and wonder
Awakening to truth, be free, for none can put asunder

Strawberry looked at daisy still asleep upon the ground
Her bed a leaf of mother's tongue, each side of knife, extremes are found
But daisy had a love that's true and showed her stripes that very day
When she declared war on a witch, prepared to give her life away

Strawberry closed her eyes and once again she felt the two embrace
Unconditionally loving sisters, found within a race
So many bridges, walls and wires, trap and tie the wrong thoughts down
Nowhere can you find the answers stuck inside a foreign town

She opened up her eyes and saw that daisy's eyes were open too
Each felt the glow inside their hearts, so natural, not a thing to do
To see the love that's all around, akin to that that's found in mind
Suggests a change is truly made, to see as though a different kind

"As lovely as this moment is, I must insist you listen now"
Each fairy heart then skipped a beat as roy the rat bent down to bow
"Oh sorry darling fairies both, I didn't mean to scare you so
But i've some information for you, something that you both should know"

"A message from a bird on high, an eagle owl so wise and bold
Within his grasp of talons sharp, the secrets here for you unfold
Well, just at least the ones you need, the ones to help you on your way
Progress, communicating blue, a hue as seen on brightest day"

With that he stopped, he picked a tooth, he looked to each, he seemed aloof
He looked beyond, then left, then right, looked up and saw receding night
"Well then, i'll be on my way, consider all you see this day
The easier the path, it's true, the right path you have found for you"

"For talk of struggle, sacrifice, to me these things don't sound so nice
No need to push the waste up hill, no magic spell, no secret pill
A simple task you've always known, no need to have another shown
Just trust yourself and be your best, peace with you, enjoy your rest"

As quick as he appeared he went, not down a hole, not up a tree
For roy the rat just disappeared, and yet, is always there to see
No, never gone, he stays in words, the words that linger in your mind
To poke and prod and goad you on, towards the truth you're so inclined

Strawberry angel seemed to frown, a quizzing look upon her face
All thoughts of old they can be found, and so her mind begins to trace
Daisy sits, to watch her face contort like rubber ball in hand
Her head bobs up and down then further, left and right, like ship unmanned

Strawberry raised a finger on her hand, as though to scream and shout
Then frowned and bowed her head again, there's nothing there, so nothing
out
Daisy placed a hand upon her arm and smiled "it will come"
"I know, I know", said strawberry angel, "maybe when we see the sun"

Again each closed their eyes to rest and build the life force energy
And like all others on a quest, fell into mind and down the tree
How many times the blind can see the love and all they need to do
Perhaps they are afraid to see the simple truth they always new

How many times must we be told a simple way to reach and see
A constant toil, based on passion, take a breath and one, two, three
Nothing more to say or do, except remind you of the same
The catalysts are always working, do we really know the game?

33

T ap tap tap, the bang on window, tap tap tap, the noise again
Tap tap tap, it just continued, drive a normal man insane
In the half light of the morning, peeking through a slit of eye
Could not believe what he was seeing, had to blink, to clear his eye

Perched upon his window sill and nearby on a branch of tree
The crooning crows prepared for singing, clearing throats and sipping tea
Klaus, who didn't do the mornings, rattled forward on his chair
Guinea pig's a little grumpy, crooning crow's began to stare

They watched in silence, watched him get up, angry face, from comfy chair
All his clothes they seemed so wrinkled, messy desk and messy hair
Slowly creaking open windows, one by one he pulled them back
Slowly peeled his lips apart, prepared his teeth for full attack

"Don't you know what time it is, any of you got a clock
Even understand the measure, understand the tick and tock?
This is what I call a window, picture it, for me to see
There's the ruddy door you come in, bugger off and drink yer tea"

"If you disturb me when I slumber, one more time, you'll get to know
How razor sharp I keep my teeth, you got it now? right, off you go!"
He slammed the windows closed and pulled the curtains over one by one
Hadn't slept well, needs more time, and so blocked out the rising sun

The crooning crows had flown to village green, with not a single sound
And once were there began discussing things together, huddled round
"Quite rude, I thought", said boris stiffly, "not what I expected, no
Not as nice as that young bean with all 'is secrets there on show"

"I liked the bean" said bob; bill nodded, "yeah, a really lovely guy"
"Alright ladies, knock it off, you'll have me wiping tear from eye
This contract pays a decent crust, its easy work, the hours are short"
"What? day and night? you must be joking!"; "sorry, lost me train of thought"

Boris, bill and bob continued talking 'til the sun was up
Flew back when the pub was open, grabbed a bite, a drink to sup
They waited there until were summoned, summoned up to see the pig
Would he be in better mood, enough to dance a little jig?

The news they had, it wasn't bad, but then it wasn't really good
They always did as they were told, like coming back, just as they should
To share the goings on near solsbury, tell about young al the bean
Talk about a special mission, sophie? maybe she's his queen

Klaus, he listened, patient, rested, let it all sink in his brain
Tried to find the hot potatoes, flush the rubbish down the drain
"Tricky stuff, this new beginning, waking up the higher mind"
All discovered, based on purpose, no success for those unkind

Klaus paced up and down his office, "strawberry, daisy, compass, bell
Now the witch has gone an' wrecked it, feel as though i'm nearing hell
Who's the bean and what's he after, is it he that I should seek?
Does he know the hidden secrets, could I find the time to peek?"

He ventured out through door of office, stood on landing high above
"Someone go an' shout for morris"; someone answered, "on it, guv"
That someone went outside the pub and shouted down the morris hole
It always caught the mole's attention, even in a sleeping hole!

"Crows get back an' watch that bean, an' watch his lady friend an' all
Anybody heard from freddy, where's that 'witch' list from the wall?"
Someone brought him sheets of paper, naming every witch they new
Every year they found another, every year the list, it grew

Klaus looked at the wedge of pages, fanned and flicked but didn't look
Felt the weight of knowledge present, thought it could become a book
"Take these down to glandwey goblin", Klaus then scanned the hoard below
"Glandwey have a look at this lot, you might see a witch you know"

"I call it 'Which Witch', seems quite catchy, I might publish later on
See if you can spot her mug shot here amongst these lovely swans
Take your time, this is important, once you're through, go through again
Can't afford mistakes now can we; me? they all look just the same"

Klaus strode back into his office, "when he gets here send him up"
All knew he was meaning morris, treats him like a favourite pup
But morris, well, was sort of different, thought of things in different ways
Never seemed to judge too quickly, deep in thought for many days

Morris also had an insight into worlds most cannot see
Changing worlds of different colours, find the balance, set you free
"Morris, he'll bring news of something, more insightful than the rest"
Klaus fell fast asleep in chair, his fingers resting on his chest

~*~

34

"Morris!"; "just a little longer"; "MORRIS!"; "just five minutes, please"
"MORRIS!"; "what's that?" through his bleary eyes, "ATCHOO!", a morris
sneezed
As well as giving space to run, the cosy resting pockets found
Here, young morris mole was sleeping, over-sleeping, underground

Such a space for sound to rumble, wave on wave, vibrations track
Sound, the very first beginning, co-creation fills the sack
Awareness folds the fabric of creative mind to bring anew
A universe, dimensions full, a place to grow for me and you

And sound we see, it is so useful, waking up the morris mole
Seems he found the rest he needed, sleep, it seems, awareness stole
To take awareness from the body, *be awareness* where it lay
Onward while the shell is sleeping, all the hours in your day

Morris took a moment to begin to see awareness new
Another day begins this morning, what a lot of things to do
A 'lick 'n' spit' across his fur, a brushing down of hands and feet
Well, paws of course on morris mole, a clean of whiskers, "there, complete"

He realised he had slept much longer, so much longer than he meant
Goes to show just what is needed when you find your power spent
But now with vital health restored, his time for klaus he could afford
And so with news of hues of green, from all directions it would seem

He trekked upon a moleway round that formed his pathway underground
And as he went he thought some more of all the things he felt and saw
What was this gift that he could see, perhaps a sign for you and me?
And those who seek, *for seekers find*, the *all* if *heart* is so inclined

As always then, while on his way, a token snack may come his way
A bug, a beetle, maybe more, all wall of moleway acts as door
and so a pause, a grab, a crunch, it seems he found some early lunch
The time ticks on, but klaus will wait, cos morris mole is his best mate

Eventually he reached his goal, the pub above which office stood
He closed the trapdoor on his hole, a simple structure made of wood
Dusted off his fur a bit, a 'lick 'n' spit' across his head
In to share with klaus his friend, the latest colour on the thread

He walked inside the house of more, the carnal trough of all the poor
the poor with time and riches too, and those with nothing left to do
Some sad, some laughing, angry, more, aroused by moving, creaking door
A stupor creeps to cover head, a table top becomes their bed

The barman motioned up the stairs and morris mole began the climb
He shot a glance to all below and thought of all the wasted time
"The time to be aware and free, and building moleways just like me"
One final look, their purpose lost, 'tis sad to choose a heavy cost

He reached the door of klaus his friend, good manners meant he had to knock
And so, as grandpa standing proud, began to sound a 'toc, tic toc'
A sound of music from within, a gentle sound, he scratched his nose
A little pause to stay in time, he kept the beat with all his toes

"Come in", a voice melodic rang, that seemed to share a note or two
The music playing sweet and gentle, what it was he'd not a clue
"Well bless my soul, it's morris mole, yes morris mole it is, it's true!
My dearest friend, so good to see you, come to share then, something new?"

"I have, I have, the things i've seen, in all directions going green
The buzz, the vibe, the change in hue, but under solsbury hill its new!"
Klaus was popping, eyes were wide, excitement he could hardly hide
"Slowly morris, take a seat, explain it all with facts complete"

"Perhaps before we start, some lubrication, I could get a round
A sort of celebration of the next big clue you've gone an' found
The usual then for both of us, i'll order now, the normal trick"
He crashed his foot upon the floor, "two lemonades, and make it quick!"

Morris grinned and shook his head, "you're such a rogue"; "i know", klaus said
"You've got to keep 'em on their toes, it's true, as everybody knows
You give an inch and they'll take two, it's quite a common thing to do
Things are changing, not the same, and manners? well, it's such a shame"

On the door a knock, and "enter", in the barman came with tray
"There you go your royal highness, lemonade, the first today"
"Sarcasm, i'll tell yer now, 'tis said, the lowest form of wit
And if yer gonna use a title, next time bow you dozy twit"

The barman put the drinks on table, winked at morris, walking out
Morris put his hand in pocket, "no, no morris, it's my shout
You know you never have to pay for anything you get from me
It's only species, size and colour, stops us being brothers, see?"

"Now tell all about what happened, when it happened, tell me all
Every bit of information, big and detailed, really small"
They talked for over ninety minutes, morris told him all the news
From all the colours seen to date, and even told him of his snooze

The more he said, the more von stroodle seemed to be intrigued
So many clues, expanding base, more characters, where will it lead?
So many bits of paper, scrambled notes and bits of map
It really was a big conundrum, 'fire 'n' brimstone', such a trap

"Without the compass, is it over? just what is the role it plays?
Time is running out, I know, it's done and finished in three days
Two of them have gone already, is there something i've not done?"
"Klaus, you're doing all you can, we'll see more truth in rising sun"

"Morris, you're a pal and no mistake, you lift me when i'm down
You fill me full of hope you do, i'm always glad when you're around"
"I'll be off then", morris said, "i know there's more to feel and see
Just close your eyes and rest a bit, you might just see that stuff like me"

Morris smiled and left the room, "i'll see you mate", he gave a wink
Drained his lemonade and turned, patted out on limbs of pink

Klaus sat back in comfy chair and thought of all the things they'd talked of
All the drawings, all the notes, all the things they thought and said,
It wouldn't be that easy, resting, trying to find the forty winks
His brain it seemed was almost buzzing, so much going through his head

Glandwey, she was still downstairs, fanning through the witchy pics
Couldn't see a likeness, no, but loved to read of all their tricks
Her dogs received her thoughts conveyed about the tricks, she wants them all
And so she co-creates disaster, sets herself up for a fall

No shortcuts, the toil and labour, jobs to do and minds to set
Not a task to take on lightly, not for broadcast? not for bet!
Understand your own position, same as everyone it seems
Same illusion, same confusion, sleep's for seeing, not for dreams

~*~

35

Freddy falcon hovered as his eyes they scanned the meadow floor
Watch for bodies, liquid trails, the hunter seeks to kill a score
"There you are my little beauty, just a snack, a little vole
Maybe later i'll get lucky, catch myself a 'morris mole'"

Darting down, increasing speed, just like a rocket, fired and freed
And 'crash' his talons/feet, an' awl, pinned down a vole amidst the sprawl
Flew off and landed back in tree, where molly mouse, she waited still
And peeled her eyes for signs of life, signs of life upon the hill

What she saw; she shrieked in horror, gasped as though a knife plunged in
"Vinnie! that's my cousin, vinnie, you've just gone an' done 'im in!"
Freddy's face it turned to horror, eyes as wide as they could be
"Madam, please, i'm trying to eat, count your lucky stars you're free"

Freddy's beak began to rip and tear the flesh of languid vole
Lifeless wonder, served a purpose, as all life upon this land
Understand the one connection, then connect with single goal
Life comes easy, part of nature, have a care what's in your hand

Molly mouse was tough for sure, was not your average rodent, no
She was made of stouter stuff, necessity had made her grow
But life in any form is precious, though we see our nature's way
Testing times, to overcome them, that's our task then, come what may

Molly climbed along the branch and moved away from terror found
Up the tree a little higher, seeing further over ground
Glancing back, she saw the terror, saw the bobbing of the head
Pictures in her mind were forming, caused a shiver from the dead

Molly mouse, she reached a point where all around a line could draw
To turn three sixty full degrees and mark where sky had kissed the floor
No sense could ever fail to see the beauty then of such a sight
And feel that beauty crucified when just the same is seen at night

The little points of love and light, the countless wonders love me true
With all the planets spinning round, unseen in all their states and hue
It *all* was there for her to see, if she would but descend the tree ...

~*~

36

Strawberry angel, darling fairy, also daisy fairy too
Had rested for so long, it seemed they'd both forgotten what to do
As luck would have it, always found, a *catalyst* will bring you round
They simply opened eyes to day and blue engulfed in every way

With all the green and blue around, the light and love of sun above
Within a beak, a plant to feed, brought forth upon the wings of dove
And here, for fairies numbered two, a catalyst would come to chat
As if by magic, daisy said "well bless my soul, it's roy the rat!"

"Good morning ladies, delicate and wondrous creatures that you are
Is there a purpose to my presence? from our homes we've strayed so far
And yes, I can attest to all the thoughts now running through your head
And also, you can bless your souls, I think that's what young daisy said"

"But that's enough of non-sense, as it's all well... simply based on thought
No, sorry, that's the wrong way round, so simply, all the lies are bought
No guile and no deceptions ever, not when coming from your heart
At the top is something waiting, maybe you two should depart?"

Then as he flashed from out of view as quickly as he came
An echo rattled round the stones, and to their ears some truth it came
"Onward ladies, fairies all, take out your wands and hold in hand
Now stake a claim on all you love and everything will go as planned"

"For magic, it is simply love, there's nothing that it cannot do
It leads you on to top of hill, on silbury all around is blue
And there a key you'll know and use, the single tone of fairy bell
Unlock the sound of earnest heart, then all the secrets, *all* will tell"

~*~

Here another thread is woven, woven then as part of fate
Going round and round in circles, why defer it? keep it straight
Finding then your true direction, single, simple path for all
Seen as one with mother nature, in the sunlight standing tall

Flutterbys and buzzy bees, sticks an' stones we're all the same
Simple hints from someone knowing, what's the difference in a name?
study, study, all as ordered, know it all? it keeps you lame!
Wonders then, the most deluded, those that play the science game

Strawberry, daisy, then set off to reach the top of silbury hill
Common sense is there among them, truth is such an easy pill
Swallow, swallow, down it goes, to bethlehem, a house of bread
Save each month we must the first born, 'al k'line' won't see it dead

A temple made without the sound of hammer, drill or even saw
One that's mobile, in the billions, cannot enter through a door
Light will never stream through windows, filling body full of light
Not unless you search in earnest, single eye in dark of night

~*~

138

37

139

Boris, bill and bob, the crows, had been around the house a while
When out into the garden came an al the bean with beaming smile
He sat upon the very chair they'd seen him on the day before
When they all jumped upon his knee and knocked each other on the floor

For just a moment all he did was take in all he saw around
He shifted in his seat a bit and planted bare feet on the ground
He rested easy in his chair, he didn't seem to move too quick
With all his movements purposeful, sit up with comfort, that's the trick

He scanned around the garden floor and smiled at all the things he saw
Representing all the work of mother nature's hand
Built with nothing more than love, on a scale beyond the grand
For nothing here that nature builds, devoid of purpose, so fulfilled
Each tiny chemical so small, like atoms making up a wall
The links that make a special chain, we like to label dna

Feeling full of love from all the wonder that he'd seen
He closed his eyes, took three deep breaths and journeyed to a land serene
Darker, deeper, deeper down, beyond a place of noise and sound
To find a place of higher you, the one that knows all you can do

And so, he found a place to grow, to balance colour as we go
A place where just the single vibe, began the *all* and made our tribe
Twas under sun and sky that day, another also found their way
Reflected on the trio true, the sky communicating blue

~*~

Boris, bob and bill, the crows, had watched the bean come out and sit
Partly hid by branch and leaves they sort of bounced around a bit
"We gonna stay?", asked bob of boris, "gonna have a chat with him?"
"It wouldn't hurt", said boris, "though the last time it was just a din"

"But that was after we all jumped, because he talked to us before
Remember he was sort of sparkly, feet, they didn't touch the floor"
The boys remembered, beaks a nodding, all concurred that they should stay
Maybe they could ask more questions, what the bean will do today

And so the crows, they watched and waited, waited then for al the bean
Was this then a day of balance moving on to blue from green?
All for each is then a wonder, nothing more for each to do
Simply breath to find the silence, in the darkness born anew

Often hearing words of wisdom, vacant gazes on the face
Sad so few will pause and listen, just a choice, there's no disgrace
For none so blind as those that see, and all they see, to them is true
The contrast stark, beyond illusion, think there's nothing they should do

Singing songs, repeating words, and yet, no understanding found
They stay as ape, a beast contented? dragging all along the ground
To think, I am, and so you are, but there you stop and see no more
Your minds and thoughts are all of you, the ego chains you to the floor

To dare to see a fragile you, a simple you, a child you
A you that understands and dreams of all, cos all is so much more
Than simply shouting "look at me, I thought and did, there is no more!"

And so, the illustrations of another may be found
To demonstrate an inner way of truth and light and love
To energise an earnest seeker, drag awareness off the ground
Become at one with all around, and al perceived as god above

~*~

38

In the house of gladys there are many, many games to play
The choice is yours, just take your pick, then off you go, you're on your way
Perhaps you'd like to play a board game, maybe cards or play with ball
'What's the point of games?' you ask, well only changing saul to paul!

Here we see young sophie found, her eyes are closed but not asleep
Inside is darkness all around and all she finds is hers to keep
All her thoughts dissolve to ground, not always grazing pastures new
Can the smallest voice be found, the one that's always seeking you?

Dedicated, loving, all-forgiving, merciful and kind
All her thoughts are done and dusted, what then is there left to find?
Will this seeker find a treasure, milk and honey, silver, gold?
Knowing *all*, is that a secret, kept from all and never told?

When you find the secret keep it, understand the reason why
All is for a bean to fancy, question, what's the single eye?
If you truly are of passion, of a faith that's pure and true
Words may cause a bean to seek, with open heart, it could be you!

Sophie then, had found the balance, understanding thought and deed
Found a friend in 'al k'line', to fast and help protect the seed
Cast below an eye to egypt, climb through heavens up above
Soon to greet the pharaoh's daughter, with the grace of god and love

Easily, the pure of heart will always find a way to see
The truth in purpose of the bean, embrace the dark, descend the tree
Slowly, surely, all will crumble, falling down revealing more
Love and light are always streaming, yearning souls will open door

Errors of the fearful claim the souls of men; so many know
That evil sits in hearts of beans by choice; don't say it isn't so
If truth were known would chaos reign or simply take the rein from you?
May god have mercy on your souls, all sins are yours, and that is true

To lose your fear and break the chains of every single living bean
Would then create a world unknown, the simple things, like blue and green
No covenants with gifts of love, no charge, no fee, the only way
For only here is heaven found, for each in every different way

Without, there's only reason and confusion shared as words of sound
Within, awaits infinity, and here the *all* is always found
So ask yourself, what you would do, or rather who you'd like to be
An ostrich, head stuck in the ground or flying bird with all to see?

Some will simply take a lifetime, is there really many more?
Would you risk a chance encounter, leave the knowledge at the door?
Listen to a love that's calling, trying to wake a sleeping you
Want to end the dreaming now, want to find another view?

Sophie moving on transcended, hues of green so full of love
Balanced out her thoughts intended, expectations, give a shove
Finding peace within, so easy, practised all when all is new
Fear is gone through faith, of course, now communicating blue

~*~

39

Not often is a mole seen rushing, nor, could one say, out of breath
But morris mole was on a mission, oaths to friends on pain of death
Such as what you might call old school, very hard to find today
Attention spans of seconds common, aggravation in the fray

Bursting with excitement he came bowling out the door
Where he'd come from just this minute, through the moleways on the floor
The speed was almost uncontrolled, he bounced off wall to door of pub
Crashed through the door in such a fashion, startled all those eating grub

Klaus was on the stairway leading back up to his office lair
The noise was such to halt his progress, made him look, it made him stare
"Morris, this a surprise, whatever are you doing back?"
"Hey, it's morris!" others said; "come upstairs, ignore the claque"

Klaus just spun on single foot, another met the rising tread
And as he climbed he turned to barman, had a look but nothing said
Already on the counter top, two glasses chilled with lemonade
"Keep it up, anticipation, might review what you get paid"

Klaus continued up to office; morris, settled, followed up
The barman, well, he followed morris, with two drinks for them to sup
The barman placed the drinks on table, closed the door on his way out
"Ok morris, let us 'ave it, calmly now, no need to shout"

Morris gulped some lemonade and rested back into his chair
He took a breath and then another, rubbed his paw across his hair
"Incredible... ", he said and paused, but klaus, he uttered not a word
And gave him all the time he needed, interrupting now's absurd

Gently nodding, showing he can now relax and tell it all
Morris seemed beside himself, though not perplexed, no, not at all
"I had to come and tell you of this latest change I felt and saw
It's not as simple as we think, like taking steps one, two, three, four"

"How many steps then must we take? a number's all I need to see"
"There's not a number here for viewing, steps could be infinity"
Morris told him of the colour, heard communicating blue
"It's sort of like a loop of progress, things to learn and things to do"

Morris sipped the lemonade again and took another breath
But just before a word came out, an image flashed of life and death
"Imagine if there was no time to worry of, no limits found
And what if life continued on when all these shells returned to ground?"

"Morris, morris, steady lad, yer talking nonsense, sound confused
Just take a minute, gather thoughts", poor klaus it seems was now bemused
Unusually, morris rose and there began the floor to pace
"I just feel different, different thoughts, found a purpose, different race"

"I tell you klaus, and mark my words, this time's for *you*, to also see
To what extent depends on you, it's almost like i've been set free
To say I know of something new, it isn't really right or true
When searching ever deeper down, it's something that I always knew"

"Morris, I don't understand, 'the deeper down', what do you mean?
I thought we'd find a single secret, single step, complete the dream?
You use the word infinity like something that i'll never find
I hope it's not a riddle morris, not another, that's unkind"

"Faith", said morris, "that's the message, simple faith will always do
In fact, the *will* that it inspires is all you need to carry you"
Morris mole came back to chair and supped another sip of drink
Relaxed again, he brushed his hair, so confident, with paw of pink

Klaus von stroodle sat and stared and tried to take all said inside
The truth? well he was more confused, sat mouth open, eyes were wide
Moments passed and morris simply sat with an awareness new
Of things for him and klaus to think on, things to see and things to do

"Time", said morris, "never-ending, time for us to go and see
All the magic, plenty of it, maybe it will set you free?
Fill your mind with expectation, wonders of the like unseen
Privileged we are, I tell you, yet more truth for us to glean"

"Glandwey and her dogs can take you, to the top of solsbury hill
Would you travel several hours, a curiosity to fill?"
Klaus began to screw his eyes up, tilted head this way and that
Looked around till eyes found bag, confirmed position of his hat

Neither spoke for several minutes, supping lemonade was true
Slowly creeping up on klaus, the very thing he had to do
"Morris, am I right in thinking, please correct me if i'm wrong
It's time *I* should be getting busy, time for *me* to sing *my* song?"

"And then I wonder of the secret of the sacred fairy bell
Of the quest of strawberry angel, daisy, merddyn, witch an' spell
Bertimus my top reporter, here at first, now disappeared
Uncontrolled i'm feeling morris, is it time to face all fears?"

"Glandwey goblin full of mischief, always reckless in her play
'Carnal' dogs' voracious hunger, will they all lead me... astray?
Are my yearnings all for nothing, wanting, greedy, take it all?
Fear is growing deep inside me, is there nowhere else to fall?"

Morris saw the fear, confusion, terror growing in his eyes
"You'll only hear the truth you want to, never are you hearing lies
None so blind as those that see, deceivers of the self they are
To find the truth, don't need a ticket, never have to travel far"

The pair, they sat, and morris talked of revelations, things unseen
Answered questions klaus threw at 'im, of the darkness, of the dream
Soon they'll all be thinking, doing; love will bias different ways
Slowly lift a dark confusion, clarity replaces haze

"I'll be off, i'll see you there, there's plenty more to come, I feel"
Morris turned and left the office, open wounds could now congeal
Klaus had had his little world turned upside down, upon its head
All the things we think we know, its rubbish, even of the dead

He sat and pondered what may lie ahead, this time to really see
Why moon sits high in different houses, twelve in number, then one three
What's the link of love and light and what's the deal with changing hue
It really is a simple task, and not that technical for you

"Soon, just maybe..." thought Klaus

~*~

40

Mum and mum and gladys, each a seeker of the purest way
Came out into the garden, as the sun began to end the day
In comfort all around they were, the kids had joined them too
To share a moment in awareness, shared within so deep and true

The crooning crows both in a tree and on the ground were passing time
To greet the seekers, one and all, expressing love, the form was prime
The moments passed, not very long, for often had they sung this song
A song within, expressed without, the faith complete, devoid of doubt

And one by one the crows did see; the apples fall from in their tree
And then could see this glowing form, to walk together was the norm
A social group as always found, for each is just a part of *all*
All thoughts and feeling echo round, a *social complex* has no wall

The crows, collected all together, sat upon the garden gate
Watched the beans begin to move, is every move then, simply fate?
To balance out the indigo and open gateways through the fence
Embrace the will, receive the love, *the infinite intelligence*

The light and love within the three, empowering younger ones to see
And so we see the change in hue, it runs up indigo from blue
The crows without a word can hear beginnings of a single roar
A single vibe, a perfect wave, made everything that came before

And everything will always be, the very thing we want to see
As moments in awareness roll, in loops around your very soul

Two mothers then, and gladys, danced the dance of light and flew through air
Sophie's hair as strands of light, through walls as though they just weren't there
Al the bean just nodded as he passed beyond the crows and gate
To reach the top of solsbury hill, receiving co-created fate

~*~

Some distance off was freddy falcon, molly mouse still on his back
Occasionally out on wing, to quell the boredom on attack
They watched them reach the top of silbury, sit and wait, and wait some more
no action, for no sign of bell, a change in hue, just as before

"I know what's coming next", said molly mouse with such a causal air
"Poor klaus can't open up to truth, his eyes don't see, they simply stare"
"What?" said freddy, turning head completely round from front to back
"You say you know what's coming next, yet calmly sit with not a quack!"

"I'm not a duck", said molly swift-ly (clearly though, she's not a bird)
"Not everybody screams their business, thoughts, desires, that's absurd"
Some things are simply meant for each, and each will simply find, alone
and some may never see the light, it matters not how often shown

"So tell me molly mouse, oh wise one, tell me what will we see next
For truly boredom's taking hold, the purpose? well, I feel perplexed!
To intercede before our time seems such a risky thing to do
Let's share ideas then, here and now, as you're a lady, d'après vous"

150

"Poor klaus has many, many books and drawings, things he can't perceive
It's all to do with lineage, a boy called adam, girl called eve
While they're simply symbols of a story from so long ago
All stories show the way to light and all were hid through fear, you know?"

"A lie can weigh a good bean down, the lies and tricks to con, deceive
The shameful acts of trusted beans... and what a tangled web they weave
Some books still try to show the way, some pictures clearly show the light
So many beans just cannot see the simple way to do it right"

"The ever-present order in the chaos that we all believe
Is all there really is to life, and so, ourselves we do deceive
The coloured bands, the energies, to balance each and every hue
A task of love for every bean, and such an easy thing to do"

"The problem for the beans of course, to find the faith to run alone
Takes courage and a strong belief, to search for things you're never shown
Strawberry went from green to blue, we saw the aura with our eyes
And next will come the indigo, for perfect sight, to balance lies"

"But after that, I can't remember, violet then, and maybe white?
It's also something we may see, contrasting with the dark of night
But as for golden arrow and its purpose, I just cannot tell
And never have I seen a word or picture of the fairy bell"

Freddy falcon sat there stunned, his head was tilted, wide his eyes
"Molly mouse, i'm almost speechless, you are *such* a big surprise!
Klaus is giving orders out when you're the one that sees the truth
Tell me why the silence then; both work and play, you share a roof?"

"To disagree or prove they're wrong when answers sit in front of face
Promotes their anger "*kill the wrong*"! you get the blame, and so, disgrace
With *all* he has, what does he see? still nothing; ego blocks his view
And likely 'til the day he dies, there's little someone else can do"

"Let sleeping dogs lie?" grinned freddy

"those carnal beasts never sleep", molly replied

~*~

41

The dark of night brings so much promise, so much comfort, time for rest
Respite from the day's encounters, toil and burden, all a test
Except of course, when on a mission, on a mission for a cause
Selfless are the jobs of many, little time for praise, applause

Morris, klaus and glandwey goblin, met quite near the house of bean
In the distance solsbury hill, an angel sang of journey seen
Glandwey's dogs seemed sort of restless, sloshing chops and growling
thought
Would a bean give in? distraction, helpless, as the doubt is bought

Morris mole was found a wanting, for some patience shared around
Klaus von stroodle's in a panic, truth unseen, so nothing found
"Morris you've just got 'ere mate, but i've been here since five to six
Glandwey's dog's take some controlling, always coming up with tricks"

"They got you here though, didn't they?" said glandwey goblin not amused
"Yes they did, just like I wanted, fell off twice, the ego's bruised"
Morris nodded, looked around and asked about the violet light
Klaus said "yes, we saw a change within the bands you see so bright"

Morris looked and then inspected, paced and turned and walked some more
What he said was unexpected, mentioned universal law
"...I don't know why you're so determined, here you are and so must be
On to top of solsbury, mate, there's one last thing for you to see"

"But can't you tell me what it is, you know i'll be there all alone"
"Glandwey and her dogs will take you", morris offered all a bone
"Don't you ever feed my dogs, all they need they get from him
And all the others fearful like 'im, greedy, lazy, blind an' dim"

"My, she has a way with words", said klaus to morris, winks the eye
Glandwey goblin cracked her whip, off they shot, he waved goodbye
"I'll see you at the top then morris"; "maybe, maybe not, we'll see
I really need to rest a while, put me feet up, have some tea"

Klaus and glandwey in perspective, getting smaller in the view
Noise like words, they reached his ears, but what they were, he never knew
Morris turned and walked towards the shells of bean upon the grass
Inspected them with fascination, strands connecting, looked like glass

The crows had watched without a word since klaus and glandwey had arrived
Preferring more to just observe from in the tree where they could hide
The dogs were unpredictable, in some ways uncontrollable
But always were emotional, to fuel the carnal crimson tide

Morris made his way back home and sat relaxed in favourite chair
For one last time again that day, he dragged a paw 'cross velvet hair
Inside, he had determined, was a place that he could now explore
And so as not to be disturbed, he bolted tight his own front door

He closed his eyes and sought no thought,
yet still the thoughts would come and go
Until they'd used up fizz 'n' pop, then into darkness he would grow
For when we sleep, a world awaits for exploration all brand new
Repair the body during rest, the shell has natural things to do

Indigo to violet, so subtle is the change in light
The sound above, beyond below, each in truth beyond the sight
But then, all reference I convey, for all, within the sense is bound
This very box we must escape, for only then is freedom found

~*~

42

As if by magic, magic clock, the world it spins without tic toc
The pendulums, the worlds we see, for now they hold no truth for thee
To balance moves in *out of space*, all spirals form as part of race
All energies, complete the dance, creation, man cannot enhance

Comprehend the scale of *all*, a contrast then, to all, you are
Of time and space as we perceive, in space and time, confused you are
So loved and cherished, never ending, blind to truth, it seems you are
Time for you to take a peek? a seeker then, *you* truly are

~*~

Strawberry angel darling fairy, sat atop of silbury hill
Daisy fairy close and watching, loving sister, bore no ill
Swirling specks of light within, had moved to indigo from blue
And here we see another change, beginnings of a violet hue

Never still for more than moments, nothing ever stays the same
Transformations here for all, and always then, we're in the game
Automated sequencing; within dear strawberry, process grew
And there within, as clear as day, her crown it glowed a violet hue

Freddy falcon, bored, frustrated; here, the archetypal goon
Saw the glint of hidden compass, by the light of winter moon
Without a thought or plan of action, weighing up of pros and cons
Actions of a killer, pure, never seeing right or wrongs

He launched from up on high, attack; a fearsome grin at crack of beak
A lust for blood within his eyes, just death and havoc would he wreak
Strawberry angel looming closer, talons coming to the fore
Beak begins a fearful snapping - 'WOOSH'... and freddy was no more

Molly mouse, the perfect view to see the saving of the day
An eagle owl so silent flew, on grabbing freddy, flew away
The eagle owl so big and strong, to gather bird with single claw
Then once a distance off the hill, to cast the falcon to the floor

Freddy's heart was racing, so convinced was he that he was dead
"STAY AWAY", was all he heard, as once more it flew overhead
He quickly flapped to nearest tree, to tend his wounds, his ego bruised
He'd sit the dark of night out here, this eagle owl was not amused

This eagle owl, before unseen, in dead of night, through silent air
To disappear before your eyes and leave you scratching head and hair
Though molly mouse did truly see the shift in shape to merddyn's form
With but a glance to where she sat, he silenced her with fear of cat

Around, and then around again, a hand to conjure in the space
A frame and form from heart of love, the spicks and specks and spots of light
They danced around the strawberry fair, a sleepy smile grew over face
And there begins with nothing more, the inspiration of her grace

~*~

43

Through darkened meadow, on the journey to the top of solsbury
Klaus von stroodle, glandwey and her dogs of carnal nature roared
Appearances may be deceptive; klaus of course is soft and furry
Glandwey and her dogs appear to be from some archaic hoard

But there beyond the sweetest smile, the breeding and the manners true
The sharpened teeth of blind ambition, fail to make a case for you
There is of course, no law of bean, could ever stand the test of time
For *time* itself is just illusion, sadly, man still missed the prime

And so, goes blindly on in faith, of nothing, 'cept that sense of self
Believing still, I own it all, a gun and fear, now give me pelf
And pelf is all you ever see, and more to crave the things it brings
And those that seek control of all, will find there are no angel wings

And so to here, the top they reached, and al the bean sat still and calm
Their presence here, it served no purpose, caused no fear, could do no harm
Klaus commanded dogs and goblin, ordered then and there, attack
The dogs of course, controlled all weak wills, found in every bean a lack

But al was not your average bean, true purpose had he found in life
Imperfections caused a wobble, generally, he balanced knife
His body plain, in form of light, and love so deep, in earnest true
Twas then before their very eyes, they saw the birth of violet hue

They charged the body, light and love, but many metres from their goal
A bolt of lightning crashed their path, the presence of an ancient soul
They stopped as though were frozen dead, with just their senses working on
Thoughts were racing through the mind, the dogs as always, sewed the con

Merddyn stood as rock of ages, understanding reasons why
Rarely would he interfere, just observing through the eye
"Error have you found this day, which fuelled your journey here tonight
Klaus, the dogs have no place here, they're under heel, through single sight"

"Be gone, and know the mercy of my love for all, and all you are
Most every bean, fear things unknown, like sun and moon, the love of star
You search without, and fail to see, the light of truth to set you free
And so, believe you can control, the earth, not knowing of your soul"

"How often must you fail to see, the light that shines in all of thee?
From grain of sand, to cell of eye, will truth then, always pass you by?
Be gone! again I say, now go, and contemplate your very seed
From whence you came and what it takes to germinate and so be freed"

Merddyn crashed his staff of wonder, firmly in the sod below
And in instant all were gone, except for al, with inner glow
Merddyn moved an ancient hand and cleared the clouds from winter sky
Polished face of winter moon, the sun's delight, to feed the eye

Soon the apex of the arch, the arc of moon through space and time
A moment set in time and space, to echo love, in bliss, sublime
Alone upon the hill once more, the time was nearly here to touch
The face of all that's ever been, and all there ever was, is much

And much is, then to truly see, so little understood perhaps
The blind who choose to never see, just recreating, pointless traps
Is it fair to feed the sheep, with food that never fills the hole?
That void inside that aches and pains, devoid of love, it's called your soul

~*~

44

See, it begins

Merddyn casts an eye to progress, watches over, helps thee not?
Fear? no need, all paths are journeyed, see the present, there, the plot
Though destinations be the same for union with a love divine
Two shall then become as one, each new event seems stuck in time

One last expression of desire, a good and perfect gift
In quiet contemplation one succeeds to bridge the rift
And so, the mind is set on truth, awaken then, we must
Else all the gifts from up above will surely turn to rust

It seems *there is another way;* you choose when truth will set you free
Believe and you will find your path, to thine own self a devotee
And what is *all*, when all is found, so simple, take a look around
Your many senses clearly then, are not all you will ever be
They're simply tools used by your shell, another truth for you to see

~*~

Two hills of mother nature's form, stood miles apart, in space and time
On top of each, a thought inspired, co-created here in rhyme
Strawberry angel, darling fairy, sophie alice daisy fox
Separated by dimension, each divine, in strawberry locks

Single colours, balance found, reaching up from ground to sky
Holy ghost vibrates the signal, starts connection with the eye
Book of body, paths and ways, hidden why? 'tis greed or fear?
Find the truth within yourself, now seek the quiet voice to hear

~*~

Above and in-between the two, merddyn hovered still and bright
A thousand metres from the ground, within an orb of brilliant white
With eyelids down, though seeing all, each expectation never hide
Atop each mound, reflected soul, and merddyn stretched his arms out wide

To cast all energy of light, resplendent in its majesty
Belief within the bean doth grow, all mirrors show the corpus christi
Al the bean atop of solsbury, standing in ethereal form
For such a night as this, of wonder, nothing here detached from norm

Silbury there reflecting love, as merddyn circled hand in light
To conjure up and cast to earth, the lightning veins that forked through night
Close to where the strawberry angel stood in awe of all, as seen
The lightning veins caressed the earth and formed the cage, a lover's dream

Swirling hands on either side, to conjure more, a lens of love?
One in front of each, the lover, guided by the soul above
Any distance there between them, disappeared within the lens
Was soon to focus sharp on each, a test to see if one pretends

Al the bean could see in mind, the hills, the lens, the orb, the light
A fearless form of endless faith, embraced this spectacle of night
The crackle, hiss, of light and love that forked to kiss the ground below
before the strawberry angel, caused the cage of love and light to grow

The light, it grew and formed the bars to make a cage to hold a bird
Imprisoning a single life within the bars... it sounds absurd!
The final act, to form a door, for which a lover needs a key
The seeker, with the single eye, the path to take will always see

She took the arrow, key of light, and placed it in the lover's lock
She turned to left and right she did, took two steps back and sat on rock
The iron bars that fenced the lamp, did turn at once to golden light
Then changed their form, to dance and disappear as spirals in the night

Strawberry's form was drawn into a swirling mass of light 'n' love
And she *became* the purest light, as wings became those of a dove
Strawberry fairy turned to angel, guided by her mother hand
Mother nature, ever present, watching over all the land

Within the air a window formed, a magnifier grew,
Then miles away on silbury hill, a picture formed for each of you
"Your strawberry hair, angelic beauty, fantasy of form and grace
What's this I feel inside for thee, when i'm about to start the race?"

Awareness came of one another, saw each other through the air
After battle, foe defeated, marching time, we must prepare
Saw each other through the slip, and knew just what they both must do
Intuition, faith and love, is all there is to carry you

Merddyn bowed his head to focus, conjured up the storm within
The power and the glory of the *all*, creates all happening
As on a cross, both arms arced up, his hands they crashed above his head
The sound wave rumbled o'er the land, and all was still, like all was dead

Two beams of light burst out from orb, then down, to strike the top, so still
A pathway laid from silbury's crest, through orb, back down to solsbury hill
As though on cue, the process rolled, as always, since the dawn of time
About to see the face of god, to understand the form of *prime*

Exploding from a faith within, forever more expressed without
No words are spoken, senses change, and so, unknown is fear and doubt
Like unto snake, to strike or climb, the final stage, unreferenced time
To mix and match your heart's desire, see, as you would pen in rhyme

As each arced through a ninety, from the earth, up through the sky
Then each entwined the other, as they formed the single eye
Up like snakes revolving round a pole the two did climb
Then came together, milk and honey, tears aren't here to cry

What happened then to individual? individuals all we are
Is something held within for keeping, fuel for journeys near or far?
'Tis only fear that holds you back and feeds the veil, your daily view
The racing mind, the carnal thoughts, you pause to see confusion true

~*~

45

The crows were sleeping side by side, oblivious to all, it seems
then crashing into all their worlds came klaus von stroodle, smashing dreams
Glandwey goblin and her dogs all paused before the garden gate
Of al the bean, who they assumed, had kept the secret of his fate

Yet as they paused to gaze upon the bean who seemed to dash their hopes
Enlightened, al came walking by, ethereal, unlike all popes
He paused and sat beside them all, looked sort of perched upon the wall
He smiled and they could feel his love, for saul had been transformed to paul
Klaus climbed down from chariot and joined this luminating form
And there the two just sat for moments, knowing it was all the norm

~*~

Klaus von stroodle sat defeated, pondered on one question more
Would he tell about the secret, how to find the inner door?
Boldly then, he asked the question, "tell me what there is for me
Will you speak of all you found and whisper where you hid the key?"

"Dearest darling klaus von stroodle, you've an awful lot to learn
And yet the task is oh so simple, if the truth you can discern
Error then, is just perspective, laid aside to measure truth
Each of our unique perspectives, 'made to measure' in our youth"

"Behold majestic darkened wonder, savage as you are
Awareness born of deep within, a sense doth tell thee true
For always, as the eyes have seen all things both near and far
Each sense has failed thee not, just as they're always meant to do"

"So reaching out, extending ears, be common all around
For all the whispers, lies and truths, in all these parts that do abound
The setting sun provides a moment, you can pause, consider stuff
The evidence suggests indeed, we're all the diamond in the rough"

"Think upon the lessons in awareness as they fall before you
All the things you could've done, each twist and turn, each choice we make
Infinite potential through each catalyst that falls before us
Consequences; ours in every thought and word, each act we take"

"Every path we take is different, every step we plant the same
Words through pictures, always forming, see the nature of the game
Everything is ours to own, and truly, do we have it all
Based upon our deep connection, nature loves us, big or small"

"I can't confess to knowing all, so much is yet to come
You've witnessed here my story true, bound in laughter and in fun
So what then could you take from me, to help you on your way
Nothing can or should be given, when you deem it's time to play

"Simply know, that all is love, and then you see how there can be
An infinite intelligence, available for all to see"

"To know this is a single step of many, on our journey long
A single voice, within ourselves, to sing the only common song
Though each rebirth to learn is short, to live it time and time again?
You have to wake, to make real progress, <u>else repeat the lot</u>; a pain!"

~*~

Requiem

In the months that followed, saw a mole progressing, serving all
Without a single thought of self, he served himself and had a ball
Poor old klaus he took and took but never really found
That, which so eluded him, but always seemed to be around

One dark and dreary night in winter, bitter winds blew through the air
Klaus was in his office, dreaming round in circles of despair
He heard the crash as door flew open, muffled voices from below
Gasps, a shriek, and molly screamed, klaus seemed stuck, he couldn't go

That feeling deep within his heart, a feeling never felt before
He heard the running up the stairs, the smashing open of the door
Molly stood, her eyes were filling, feeling heavy, fell to floor
Heard the feet, the shuffle moving, eyes grew wide at what he saw

Oh so slowly, really gently, several carried morris in
Others laid a blanket down in front of fire flickering
Silent, not a word was spoken, laid to warm before the fire
Morris mole was sort of sleeping, things for him seemed sort of dire

Huddled in a group, the helpers told how morris mole was found
Outside in the cold for hours, almost frozen on the ground
All he seemed to say was 'klaus', and moments later, maybe 'right?'
Another said he heard the name, but thought he said the colour *white*

Klaus just stood, he couldn't move, 'twas almost like he couldn't breath
("No, no no, this can't be morris, morris said, he'd never leave")
His thoughts, so many; mind was racing, molly went and took his hand
"Take a breath, and take a step, not everything in life is planned"

The agony, of every step to walk and face your greatest fear
We must embrace that sad awareness, losing those we hold so near
Each single little gasp of breath we catch to help us soldier on
We fight to keep the floodgates closed, yet crumble as we sing this song

And there went all at once the feelings, klaus broke down and fell to floor
The others stood in hushed respect, they'd not seen klaus like this before
"Oh morris, morris, dearest friend, whatever have you gone an' done
Whatever were you doing out, to freeze like this with setting sun?"

He gently rested paw upon the head of morris where he lay
His guts turned over many times, as more emotions joined the fray
All just stood or sat in silence, mindful of each little breath
That morris took while warming slowly, was he trying to fight his death?

Molly looked at klaus and asked him, would he like some time and space
To help him free his trapped emotions, crying then, is no disgrace
Klaus looked up and smiled at all those present; what a thing to do!
He said, "I'd like you all to stay please, *friends*, if that's ok with you"

Molly couldn't help herself, the tears burst forth from both her eyes
"Of course," and "Ahh!" were heard from others, all were taken by surprise
As for klaus he felt a tingle, little tickle under vest?
Unbeknown to him he'd grown, just a smidgen, with the best

"It's love". cried molly, through her tears, she saw that klaus just couldn't speak
It seems that love stays in us all, yet seeks to grow and take a peek
Overwhelmed, klaus just gave in, he let it go, began to wail
Morris full of love responds, and moves a paw so weak and frail

Silence fell upon the room, as klaus reached down and took his paw
"Morris?", croaked his timid voice, he'd never felt like this before
Morris moved his head a whisker, moved towards his friend he did
"Klaus", there came a tiny whisper, all in focus, there enchanted

"Morris", klaus began to crumble, both lips trembled, squeezed his paw
All around began the leaking, tears then falling onto floor
Morris mole was seen to smile, a slowly, gently forming curve
It touched with love, most every fibre, every cell and every nerve

All were swimming in emotion, as the love around it grew
Stirs another from a sleeping, just one little thing to do
"White", there came another whisper, from the mouth of morris mole
All were joined in single feeling, all their hearts old morris stole

"Yes, old friend I know and thank you, thanks so much for loving me
Helping me to understand, how it's love that sets you free"
Klaus broke down a little more, as morris fed him all his love
To then ensure the love would grow, as intended from above

Sparklings of matter popping, eyes now moving all around
Growing, forming light unstopping, blinding, had to turn to ground
A whoosh of air, a mini storm, a swirl of dust and then to see
Appeared before them merddyn's form, most all dropped down on bended
knee

"Stand before me, bend no more, be silent as I form for thee
Here a heart like few i've seen, in truth I say, it summoned me
Then seek to understand the ways of one so true, and true for all
Who opened up his heart to seeking, never, entertained a fall"

"Understand his search in colours, understand the final white
Balance each from blended others, all expressions in the light
Matter, living rocks to plants, that reach and grow, the light to find
A light that I call *limitless*, consciousness will never blind"

Morris gave a little breath, then sort of sucked to hold one in
The grip of paw began to weaken, smiled so big, was almost grin
His head in slow-mo' rolled to side, a final little breath he blew
Here lay morris mole forever, loved by many, known by few

Tears they flowed, some hugging others, molly looked at klaus with love
There he sat, a wreck unmoving, all alone, he'd lost his glove
No more looking forward to the meetings that they used to have
The strategies, the plans, the questions, all was gone, it seemed was lost
Is this the final price to pay, for klaus, is this the final cost?

Rarely would you ever see it, rarely could you hear the song
Such is love and understanding, know compassion, never wrong
Molly hushed the gathered round, and motioned to the artful seer
He responds to yearning hearts, faithful seekers all to steer

Merddyn's staff stood tall in hand and there atop, the jewel of light
A light he fashioned brighter so he overcame the dark of night
Grains of matter, seed of soul, the essence out of morris grew
Merddyn beckons unto love, and so to jewel, the essence flew

He slowly moved the staff in hand, the tip of light to arc to floor
He tore the fabric of the space, for two dimensions made a door
The light round edge of door frame grew, and there before them came to view
The perfect form of morris mole, resplendent looking all brand new

The golden white, of love's first light, the only light we ever knew
It is the consciousness we have, it forms the soul of me and you

Morris mole, he stood to see the friends in life that saw him die
And so, began to capture each, with but a look from eye to eye

A smile of warmth and love expressed, it wasn't something you could see
Of course then, all these words you hear are simply ones soliloquy

"i miss you all," said morris mole, "my life will never be the same"
He grinned a little, carried on, was now a player in the game
"To balance out each colour true, that is the game for me and you
So simple, never need for trance, your meditation fuels the dance"

"Just one simple heart's desire, just one simple yearning song
All accepted, seen as purpose, viewed with love, there's never wrong
There's only choice in your decisions, find the love, forgiveness found
The peace and power, is in acceptance, streaming love, from out the ground"

Morris turned and came a little closer to a klaus
He paused and took a final look around the little house
He reached with glowing golden paw, towards a very special friend
To illustrate the love in *all*, the one connection, never ends

This friend with whom he'd shared a life, with only time for life's adventures
Never finding time for wife, who at the end to *all, surrenders*

The very, very bestest friend, no more that one could hope to say
except "i'll love you 'til the end, we'll meet again another day"

~*~

Merddyn stood, was almost silent, all light disappeared from view
"Embrace the *all*, that is *your* difference, always then, your dreams come true
Morris served you all his life, and always entertained your dream
His love for you, your 'joi de vivre', they're things you know that go unseen"

"Morris, gave a gift to you, the gift of love, to understand
The calling of the catalyst, to see the lesson, there as planned
See, when it's your time to pass, that love's the only thing to last

That love is *all*, and *all* is *me*,

The *i*, in *you*

It's *all,* we see"

~*~

Epilogue

And so dear reader, now you know, the tale of love and light
Of why the world is here at all; that error isn't right
'Tis now within your heart you find that love displaces fear
And it's the same for all, in truth, *illumination's near*

For always when thou seeks a union, when it's based on love
You will hear a sigh contented, from our father up above
There's a special person out there, that would be a higher you
Who yearns to pierce confusion's veil and show the world a love that's true

Mark your birthday, mark the moon, and fast your way to love and light
One simple truth to set you free, never more to know of plight
Trust how simple it can be, give in to yearnings from your heart
Then know your father sits within you, never could this love depart

All your days will fill with wonder, all your hopes and dreams come true
Just give in to love, surrender, feel the power of love in you
Accept no chains, release all anchors, nothing now can hold you down
Evermore, your song is one of beauty, love *is* all around

~*~

of Merddyn

I've seen so much, so much for one, and here I sit in winter sun
To see so much in lives of bean, to guide them through confusion's dream
So many lives, so many souls, it's up and down, a cycle rolls
Pause your thought, be free to know, find your tree and down you go

Cast your eye around, about, and notice mother nature's hand
Here, your bodies formed with love, walking over all the land
Pause and think on works of bean, the things we build and make and do
'Tis all from mother nature's hand, the stuff to keep you, like brand new

Forget the chicken and the egg, beans must accept the simple truth
It's hard to pin the old man down, because our father seems aloof
Yet all the power you need is *love*, a catalyst for change
Explore your co-creative power, nothing falls outside your range

Searching, walking, eyes are closed, yet seeing all the same
So much unimportance, where's the power in a name?
'A rose is still rose', he said, whatever name you speak
Find the answer in the silence, find the truth and take a peek

Rules and regs are such a nonsense, feeds the fear, and seeks control
Understand the ways of error, find forgiveness, lose the toll
Walk your path with one emotion, that of love, a power pure
Seek the ways of one enlightened, *here,* the truth you can procure

Think of love in all encounters, as a parent of a child
Understand the need for learning, have no fear, however wild
Faith in all you do for purpose, that of learning, seek the truth
Silent knowing, celebrating, calm in love, you found your proof

I will always wander freely, for I am a soul of light
Always will I cast the seeds of hope to ease the seeker's plight
One more thing you might consider, as the days of change draw near
Knowing, means there is no panic, love all life and lose the fear

Each of us a chosen path, each incarnation full of wonder
All these things that god created, man can never put asunder
Walk and seek to lift the veil, that is confusion of the mind
Simply ask, and *it* is given, understand no bean is blind

Fare thee well young co-creators, getting ready? number four
Time and tide will wait for no bean, waves relentless on the shore
Many things are just distractions, feel your lessons, learn them well
Never fear a choice, an error; judgement? no, there is no hell

Who's to say what's right or wrong then, who's to say who can or can't?
Who's to say 'that's wrong, don't do it', who's to say 'we'll never part'?
You or i, with all our wisdom, never could we be so bold
It's no secret, find position, couldn't say that you weren't told

No one then, should judge another? truth is, anybody can
Make a choice in your behaviour, always thought as part of plan
Choosing love to be your focus, be your guide, your force, your drive
Always then, you'll find your dreams of bliss, the world will thrive

I'll leave you now, but 'fore I go, to thee once more I would remind
Infuse thyself with love dear friend, so easy then, to find inside
Unleash this power of love within the self, to radiate beyond
From deep within your new-found essence, *cause a ripple* in the pond

To simply *change yourself* then, is the only way to *change the world*
The way is clear, just search within, the truth for you will soon unfurl
Deciding to achieve this goal will quickly set you on your way
Then truly you will walk with god, and joy and bliss will fill each day

All transcended, trans-mutated, coalesced, become brand new
Letters forming words, a pattern, conjure pictures up for you
What you see, is what you get, and what you get is what you want
But what you want, it may not be the truth you need to set you free

And so, a final word I offer, strictly from my heart
To say, all things will just come good, is not *the way,* to walk in heart
For as we sow, we then will reap, so change your ways and follow true
A life of love and dedication, to *your* cause that's pure and true

So many think, another's blood will save for all their deeds of woe
But now in truth I do reveal, to say to *you* this isn't so
The child refuses to commit to all the things, as is said and done
And choose to live a life of pleasure, revelling in *carnal* fun

You've now been told again it's true, to take the reins controlling life
Your own reflection shows the cause, dissatisfaction found, is rife
Take care in all the words you weave, to make your tapestry complete
The choice, as always, rests with you, the time draws nigh, you are replete

If you should choose to carry on exactly as you are
And realise not, the chance to learn, is moving on, so very far

All progress lost, like paradise, ignoring truth to set you free

The energy of all you are, is all that you will ever be

~*~

... the beginning

www.ingramcontent.com/pod-product-compliance
Lightning Source LLC
Chambersburg PA
CBHW070955180726
48291CB00004B/1304